Young Sherlock Holmes

ALAN ARNOLD

Young
Sherlock Holmes

DRAGON
GRAFTON BOOKS
A Division of the Collins Publishing Group

LONDON GLASGOW
TORONTO SYDNEY AUCKLAND

Dragon
Grafton Books
A Division of the Collins Publishing Group
8 Grafton Street, London W1X 3LA

First published in Great Britain by
Dragon Books 1986

First published in USA by Pocket Books,
Simon & Schuster, Inc., New York 1985

ISBN 0-583-30942-9

Printed and bound in Great Britain by
Collins, Glasgow

Set in Times

"A boy's will is the wind's will,
And the thoughts of youth are long, long thoughts"

Longfellow

Chapter One

ONE NIGHT DURING THE WINTER OF 1870 A WEALTHY London accountant of exemplary character leapt to his death through a third floor window at his apartment in Pimlico. Inevitably, in their accounts of the tragedy the newspapers made use of the term "mysterious circumstances," but their speculation went no further. Whatever terror had impelled the unfortunate man to make so spectacular an exit from life left no clue as to its nature.

There had been no break-in. The police found no evidence of foul play. It must be recorded that some patrons of a nearby restaurant recalled that he had shown signs of a lack of sobriety while dining there that evening, though no one who knew him believed that he was a heavy drinker. Indeed at the inquest, family and friends testified that he had every reason to feel life had been good to him and he had every intention of continuing to enjoy whatever years might be left to him—he had just turned seventy. Given such testimony to so blameless a lifestyle, what else could the coroner do but record a verdict of suicide? Mr. Bentley Bobster of Pelham Street had taken his own life "while the balance of his mind was disturbed," a phrase commonly resorted to in such cases, since it neatly cloaks the inexplicable. When the truth about Bobster's last hours eventually emerged it would be seen how cogent a phrase that really was.

I must state now that it was in no way due to the police that the truth came to be uncovered, although they took full credit for it at the time. No, the circumstances surrounding the demise of Bobster would be hidden to this day had the matter rested with the police. It was the result of the persistence of one singular individual, someone I was destined to meet merely days after that curious event and who would profoundly influence my life. I refer, of course, to that deductive genius, Mr. Sherlock Holmes.

I am writing from another century, from the early years of the twentieth (a century in which I must confess to feeling a lot less at ease than comfortable Victoria's), and yet I can see Holmes now, bursting into Lestrade's office in New Scotland Yard (he had the rank of detective-sergeant, then) to urge him to take up the case. I can hear his vigorous voice, full of youthful impetuosity, imploring Lestrade to be less dilatory. I can recall Holmes's burning anger when that smug detective refused to take him seriously.

Well, all that was forty years ago. When I ask myself why the events of that winter still live so clearly in my mind's eye, I know that the answer is in the tricks time plays. As one's life expectation lessens, the past spreads out its folios more luminously; the peak experiences of youth shine the most brightly. Bobster's death was to prove the first strand of a tangled web into which Holmes drew me.

It would be his first case. That it was never put on record has begun to trouble me. I feel I have neglected a responsibility to a famous man who has also been my closest friend. After all, had he not once described me as his Boswell? True, he said it at a moment when he was at his most irascible, Johnsonian to a degree, but I am sure he meant it as a compliment. At the time I was showing considerable reluctance to being drawn once again into another of his adventures (the one I subsequently related in "A Scandal in Bohemia"), but I am sure it was a heartfelt plea. "Stay where you are, Doctor," he had commanded. "I am lost without my Boswell." How could one resist such a claim?

And so I feel I must play again my Boswellian role by setting down this account of the very first case in which Sherlock Holmes and I were involved. I shall begin on that cold December evening in 1870, the evening of Bobster's impending death, which the luxury of hindsight enables me to reconstruct. . . .

Although it was snowing heavily, nothing could dampen Mr. Bobster's sense of well-being as he left his Mayfair office. Locking the street door behind him, he reflected that it had been a particularly good year in the profession of accountancy. That, of course, was also a barometer of the state of the nation itself. Despite incipient Irish troubles and the apparently insoluble problem of unemployment, England was still the wealthiest country in the world. It had been made all the more supreme by the total collapse that year of

France, which had surrendered to the Prussians. Now, no power could dispute London's claim to be the financial capital of the world. Of course, there would always be those who ranted on about social injustice, and these included Mr. Gladstone. Then in his second year as prime minister, he was pursuing radical policies that many believed would harm the economy and quench the spirit of the Empire. But Mr. Bobster knew that in commerce one dealt in realities, not ideals. The plain truth was that for growth one needed cheap labour; to keep wages down one had to have a hundred or so applicants for every available job. Wild schemes, such as Gladstone's plan to make education compulsory for children to the age of twelve, did no good at all. There was no future in that sort of nonsense and Mr. Bobster believed the working classes themselves knew it. They would be uncomfortable competing with their betters.

And so as he began his walk beside the crowded thoroughfare where hansoms jostled with horse-buses in a ceaseless flow of traffic, the scene all about him seemed to confirm his theories. Along the cobbled pavement, the shop windows were dressed for Christmas. There was no sign of a sad face. The match seller greeted him cheerfully; a woman offering lavender wished him a pleasant evening. A bright lad dispensing pies cried robustly of their quality. Content, Mr. Bobster lit a cheroot and its aroma mingled pleasantly with the appetizing smell of chestnuts roasting on hot coals. It consoled him to feel that there was nothing basically wrong with the greatest city on earth.

Friends sometimes asked Mr. Bobster why at seventy he did not retire and pack it all in for an easier life in the country. They simply did not know him. He enjoyed city life and the habit of making money. To quit now would surely shorten his life. Besides, he had achieved the best of both worlds, spending working days in London where he maintained a convenient small flat and going some weekends to his house in Norfolk where his wife, never quite in the best of health, enjoyed the companionship of their last remaining unmarried daughter. Dull weekends (damnably dull, if he were honest), for so worldly and widely travelled a man as he. Therein lay the one regret which pressed upon him occasionally. He had lost touch with the friends of his youth, the classmates of his school years. He remembered their eager faces (doubtless unrecognizable now), the abundant energy they had then, and the period he had spent with a group of them under eastern skies. For among his most cherished memories was the year he had spent in Egypt with a group of his contemporaries many years ago.

Bundled up against the cold in his fur-lined coat with a stovepipe hat atop his bushy sideburns, it was easy to yearn for that golden land again, for the camaraderie he had known under the desert sun. Now that his belly sagged and his eyes were beady above puffed cheeks, it was easy to sigh for his lost youth and its enchantments. But he checked himself. Regret was for the old and unsuccessful. Mr. Bobster believed he had a lot of life left in him. What he really needed was an excellent dinner.

Should he try Escoffier's? There, a new French chef, a fugitive from the debacle in Paris, was reputedly a master. Only that morning a colleague had recommended the cuisine without reservation, giving the *cervelles en matelote* an extra special mention. Mr. Bobster's digestive juices had flowed during his friend's description of those tender calves' brains, which had been simmered in a wine stock and allowed to cool in their own liquor for serving up firm and succulent in garlic butter. A light macon would be the only acceptable accompaniment, Mr. Bobster decided. Or should he be more conservatively English and patronize Simpson's? That excellent restaurant in the Strand would probably offer a terrine of rabbit or something else as traditional and, of course, he would follow it with their irresistible cabinet pudding, a favorite of Mr. Disraeli. He considered taking a cab to the elegant St. James Hall restaurant in Piccadilly where good staple dishes were grilled bones, roast quails (when in season), or pickled salmon. He thought too of Pimms, the chophouse that had opened near St. Paul's that very year and had already become noted for its aperitifs.

While in this mood of culinary musing he almost passed Maison Panton's without a glance at their window. There a menu was displayed and Mr. Bobster told himself that it would be foolish to travel farther when this splendid little place was close at hand. He had always been well received there, and they had never failed to satisfy him. Indeed, their skill with pheasant was really very creditable. They knew precisely how long to hang the highland birds and before cooking them made sure their breasts were wrapped with bacon and a shallot reposed in the gullets. They were conscientious about their garnishes and never failed to include essential watercress and forcemeat balls. If pheasant was on their menu tonight then he would go no farther than Maison Panton's.

But Mr. Bobster was being followed. A curiously

dressed figure had emerged from an alley and had furtively pursued him. The sinister character, swathed in a flowing cloak and hooded beneath a wide-brimmed hat, had kept Bobster at an observable distance, seemingly with some dark intent. Had Bobster not been so preoccupied with the delights of the table, he might have heard above the traffic noise an unusual sound which would have alerted him to the bulky figure. For as it moved, a golden charm on a bracelet the figure wore set up a distinctive jingle. The hungry accountant had only pheasant on his mind. Just as Bobster was discerning that the dish was indeed on the menu, another odd thing happened. He felt the fleeting pain of what might have been a needle prick the back of his neck. He put the fingers of one hand there. Detecting no blood, he shrugged the sensation away and entered Maison Panton's unaware that the dark figure had shot a dart from a blowpipe at him and then vanished into the night.

Seated now in the warm restaurant, relaxed amid appetizing odours, Bobster, while waiting for his order to arrive, sipped a very reasonable Madeira. The place was busy, couples mainly, but Bobster had never believed the enjoyment of good food was necessarily enhanced by company. On the contrary, the ceremony of dinner out was better appreciated alone, seated before crisp linen and the cosseting attentions of deferential waiters. Such were Bobster's thoughts as he tied a napkin to his shirtfront and the *maître* set before him a shining salver, lifting its cover to reveal the plump gamebird. Bobster drooled. He poised his cutlery and was about to carve the first helping when a fearful thing happened. The bird came alive!

It leapt from its dish! It screeched; it snarled! It attacked him with razor-sharp claws and vicious beak! The bird savaged his face and his chest bloodying him in a mad onslaught. In vain he tried to protect himself, but the bird's attack was relentless. In terror he rose, grabbed it in his lacerated hands, and flung it to the floor. "My God!" he heard himself exclaim as he slumped back in his chair, exhausted by the fray. Only then did he realize that he was the focus of attention. Diners, waiters, and even the cooks from the kitchen were staring at him with expressions of incomprehension. This angered him. They had seen what happened. He had fought for his life. Yet there was no sympathy in their stares, just puzzled resentment. Then he realized that the pheasant was on its dish again. He examined his hands. No scratches. His clothes were not dishevelled. Everything was quite normal. Except for the expressions which met him on every side, there was nothing to suggest that anything unusual had occurred. Embarrassed now as much as frightened, he rose from his table and left.

By the time he got home, Mr. Bobster had regained some composure. He suspected he had been the victim of an hallucination. Thinking of the scene he had made brought a nervous chuckle. The diners at Maison Panton's were still recovering, no doubt, for the English find it difficult to excuse such lack of control in public, especially in the presence of the lower orders. The waiters, of course, would conclude that he had been drunk. He began to feel a shade better.

Nervousness returned when the sturdy pair of stone horses which stood on plinths at each side of his stairway, so familiar he seldom noticed them, seemed now to threaten him. He got to his front door and inserted his latchkey. Suddenly the keyhole became a gaping mouth with teeth intent on devouring him! It snapped at his hand. He screamed. It began gnawing at his arm. Yet when he had struggled free, shocked beyond measure, he could see no mouth, no bloodied hand, only a perfectly ordinary keyhole. He had not been hurt. Everything was normal.

In a cold sweat, Mr. Bobster entered the flat and locked the door behind him. The familiarity of his room helped to calm him. The lamps from brass wall sconces spread a comforting glow. Even the ornate mahogany clothes stand on which he hung his hat and coat exuded reassurance. At last he was safely home. He splashed his face in a water bowl and towelled himself in front of a mirror. As he did so, he saw his hat sail through the air and come to a perfect landing on his head. This was too much! Who was playing such bizarre games? Mustering every reserve of control, he returned to the hat stand, replaced his hat, and with a contemptuous shrug, turned away. But not before two of the arms of the hat stand had reached out and wrapped themselves around him. In an extreme of terror he struggled, but the tentacles increased their pressure and were joined by two more, which secured his throat in a stranglehold. Now he could not even scream. Moreover, the arms of the wall sconces joined in the attack. Each arm held a fireball, which it jettisoned into the room. One landed on his bed, another in a closet. They were followed by others until fireballs were landing in all directions. Soon his flat was engulfed in flames. With a superhuman effort, Bobster broke free. He had to get out. But the door was burning and the only way was through a window. Mr. Bobster jumped, shattering the panes and landing on the icy pavement. He hit it with an appalling thud. Mr. Bobster was dead. Once assured of this, a cloaked figure fled around a corner—to the accompaniment of a curiously haunting jingling sound.

Chapter Two

I WAS SIXTEEN THAT YEAR AND HAD BEEN AT SCHOOL in Carlisle, just south of the Scottish border. This unfortunate establishment, never well endowed, had finally succumbed to a mountain of debt and unpaid fees. When it closed, my father decided to send me to the Brompton School in London, at South Kensington, about which he had received a good report from a friend. Who that friend was I was never to know, but I am entitled in hindsight to conclude that he was no judge of academic institutions.

My ambition was to follow in my father's footsteps and become a doctor; it was hoped that Brompton would equip me for future medical studies at the University of London. That this actually came about the reader may ultimately decide was more in spite of my years at Brompton than to the dubious benefits I derived from them. From the outset my studies were jeopardized not merely by a generally low standard of tutorship but by the company I kept.

I make the latter point with some misgiving because,

looking back, I realize that to have known Sherlock Holmes as closely as I was fated to do was a singular privilege, even though there were times when I cursed his excruciating self-centredness and crass egotism. But I did go to university, graduating in 1878 as a fully fledged doctor of medicine. I became an army surgeon attached to the Fifth Northumberland Fusiliers and later the Berkshires, with whom I served at the fatal battle of Maiward (1880), the scene of a bloody defeat of the British by Ayub Khan.

I have written of this in my reminiscences (*The Reminiscences of John H. Watson M.D.*, late of the Army Medical Department), published in 1882 under the title "A Study in Scarlet." I related there how in that battle I was struck on the shoulder by a Jazail bullet which shattered the bone and grazed the subclavian artery. I would surely have fallen into the hands of the murderous Ghazis had it not been for the courage of my orderly, who threw me across a packhorse and succeeded in bringing me safely to the British lines.

For months my life was despaired of until finally I rallied at the base hospital in Peshawar. Eventually I was despatched in the troopship *Orontes*, landing a month later at Portsmouth with my health irretrievably ruined. My parents having died, I had neither kith nor kin in England. Reluctantly, I decided there might be better prospects for a medical man in London, a city which, since my schooldays, I had regarded as a cesspool into which all the idlers of the Empire were irresistibly drained. I stayed for several months in a private hotel in the Strand, leading a comfortless, meaningless existence on an inadequate pension. But, of course, all that and the subsequent years with

18

Holmes at 221b Baker Street are past history. Yet on that bleak December afternoon when I arrived in London to join Old Broms (which was what we more familiarly called that establishment for the education of the sons of the professional classes), it was, of course, in the future.

In those days it would be true to say that I was rather a podgy boy. I am still what you might call rotund, but rotundity in one's sixties is hardly a matter for comment. It even enhances an air of solidity. But in a schoolboy it is not to his advantage. I was also short in stature, with a mop of brown hair which no pomade invented has ever been able to control. I consider the matter of my appearance important enough to mention because it may help my reader to appreciate my general disposition. For the popularity I could not hope to achieve through physical allure I believe I generated through good nature, amiability, and an ability to appreciate the worth of others.

I confess too that my habit of "snacking" had not helped my physical appearance. From early boyhood I had liked to nibble things, childish, perhaps, yet infinitely tranquilizing under stress. I recall that even on that maiden voyage to Old Broms I indulged myself with the purchase from a street vendor of some freshly baked custard tarts. I can savour them now, the tang of the nutmeg in the creamy egg custard; I have retained an inordinate fondness for them through life. (At Baker Street Mrs. Hudson, our housekeeper, occasionally baked me a supply, unknown, of course, to Holmes.) Snacking, then, has contributed to my pneumatic tyre and an appearance of wearing clothes always a shade too tight for me. But it has been an infallible morale booster.

However, this was not my major preoccupation on that first day in London. I was dreading the prospect of living in the vast city. Even as a boy, my nature was that of a countryman and I was already missing Northumbria's expanses and the sweet scent of its woodlands. To my unconditioned nostrils, London stank putridly of drains, sweat, chimney soot and horse dung, and it was unbearably noisy. Broughams, drays, and horse-buses (male passengers on top, exposed to the elements, the women huddled inside) jostled for space in the traffic-choked streets. Looking through the windows of my swaying, snow-lashed conveyance, the full horror of the place struck me. It was the greatest of all cities and yet it was essentially corrupt. Ragged children huddled under stone ledges, their features forlorn, pained by the cold. Apple and muffin vendors and other itinerant traders sheltered themselves from the snow beneath makeshift awnings, while the privileged competed for hansom cabs. Here and there across viaducts and bridges, engines belching smoke passed above us in disdain for the human condition.

Indeed, from copies of *The Times* which my father never failed to mail to me after he had finished with them (minus always, I noted, the obituary column in which perhaps as a medical man he took a professional interest) I had learned much about the capital's perils and its horrific incidence of accident and crime. People were crushed by horses; or they plunged off roofs and fell down shafts in this city of rampant excavation and construction. They were run over by steam engines and swallowed up in furnaces. From the Thames the bodies of Londoners were retrieved at a rate of almost a hundred a month, usually with their throats cut!

Murder and abduction were so commonplace that statistics were not kept. There were over 36,000 known criminals whose photographs were in police files and a far greater number whose faces were unknown to the authorities. Burglary and street robbery had reached record proportions, accounting for yearly property losses of over a million pounds.

Secret societies flourished, mainly for illegal ends, from anti-Czarist fanatics intent on harassing Russian refugees settled miserably in the slums of the East End, to the opium-smoking brotherhoods of Chinatown. I had read that in the poorest sections and squalid alleys of dockland, drunken men and degraded women fought for food for their starving children and that if light penetrated their overcrowded tenements, it was from the cheapest of whale oil lights flickering in the noxious gloom. In the largest and richest city in the world, of its four million inhabitants, less than half had regular legitimate employment. Even with my pride in the Empire I could not help but reflect sometimes that the working classes of this treacherous, violent city paid a terrible price for the glory and wealth their country had acquired. For all that, nothing could have prepared me for the adventure that lay ahead or the extraordinary individual who would change my life.

My carriage drew up beside an ancient archway that formed the entrance to the college. It enclosed the lodge and led to a quadrangle blanketed in snow. The solemn antiquity of the place accentuated my forebodings. I tried to cast them off as the driver discharged my luggage. After all, this was only a school. Yet I knew something of its chequered history. A Plantagenet (Henry VI) had commissioned the earliest of the buildings as a school for the underprivileged. Its success caused the gentry to usurp it and for a century their offspring boarded there. Cromwell closed it down amid rumours of degeneracy. Additions to the original structure reflected its subsequent uses. It had been at various times a hospice for the dying, a military barracks, and a debtors' prison. At the outset of the nineteenth century some Catholic families, suffering prejudice from protestant establishments, banded together to form the present school, naming it for its geographic proximity to the Brompton Road and the famous Oratory. Of course it could not compare with Eton or Harrow or Winchester in prestige, but it had sent its fair share of youngsters to death or mutilation in the punitive wars of the Empire. It had also produced a cardinal, several parliamentarians, and recruits to the East India Company, as well as a general and an over-zealous missionary whom the natives of New Guinea cooked and ate! Perhaps, I wryly reflected as I followed the porter inside, this latter fact was the basis of my father's esteem for the school; a lifetime in medical practise had driven him to agnosticism!

I followed the porter across a huge entrance hall in which an immense grate, lavishly laid with logs, had not been lit. Ornately framed canvases of far-flung battles were receding into a patina of grime. Mirrors, steamy in the chilled air, were hung so high they reflected only each other. Glass-fronted cabinets were stacked aggressively with sporting trophies and weaponry. A forlorn elk's head meditated from below a gallery. Beside some medieval armour a display of tribal headdresses, looted in Africa, looked especially out of place.

We climbed the three tiers of a stone stairway and

came to a corridor on whose walls were plaques commemorating those fallen in several centuries of wars. A sign directed us to a dormitory named for the duke of Wellington. This proved to be a long, low-ceilinged room whose rectangular shape and cross-beams suggested it was the oldest part of the building. The arrangements within confirmed this. Indeed I believe even that popular novelist, the late Mr. Charles Dickens (who had died that June), could not have conceived of a schoolroom more Spartan. On each side were small metal beds a few feet apart. A chair and a small desk stood beside each, and the effect was one of depressing uniformity. Several students were present, each identically clad in a black suit and a shirt with a white wing-collar. Some were studying, and some conversing, but none was sufficiently occupied to avoid giving me a searchingly inquisitive stare. I found my bed and sat on it. I felt exceptionally downcast. They were a dispiriting lot.

Their scrutiny continued as I unpacked, but I feigned insensitivity to it. This was made easier because my own curiosity had been aroused by the chaotic state of the bed and desk next to mine. Every available inch was taken up by an extraordinary assortment of items. There were several phials of chemical crystals, a Bunsen burner, some dog-eared newspaper clippings, a microscope, accessories for makeup and disguise, a pile of sheet music, and many books, most of them related to mystery and crime. I was pleased to note that the stories of Edgar Allan Poe were among them, because during a school vacation I had spent some gratifying hours writing an essay on the life and work of this fascinating author. Whomsoever was the occupant of this space obviously had spread his interests over a wide spectrum including, it seemed, the possibility of flight, since on the walls he had placed prints of Leonardo da Vinci's sketches for a proposed flying machine.

I was pondering this intriguing muddle when I became aware that someone in the room was playing a violin. I say *playing* a violin, but this is too complimentary. Whoever was applying horsehair to catgut was producing quite an earsplitting sound. I turned to look for the source of this abomination. Seated at a music stand merely feet away was a boy I deemed to be a year or two my senior. He was wrestling with the instrument as if it were intent on choking him. I was impressed by his appearance. His eyes were sharp and piercing, his nose thin and hawklike. They gave his whole expression an air of alertness and decision. His chin had the prominence and squareness that mark the man of distinction. I noted that his hands were blotted with ink and stained with chemicals but were obviously possessed of a greater delicacy than his prowess with bow and instrument reflected. There was a casualness about his attire. A white silk shirt, unbuttoned from neck to waist, hung loosely over his black-striped slacks and lent a Byronic touch to his appearance. The overall impression was one of restless energy both of body and mind. Suddenly he leapt to his feet and in a fit of extreme impatience opened a window; he seemed on the point of hurling the violin through it.

"Stop!" I cried.

He paused and for the first time noticed me. I pointed to the violin.

"Isn't it valuable?"

His eyes were defiant. "What is more important—the violin or my sanity?" he demanded irritably and

24

gave me no time to reply. "I should have mastered the damn thing by now."

"How long have you been playing?"

"Three days."

I was amused. "Well, perhaps you should be patient."

"Patience is a waste of time," he snapped, then relented. "But maybe you're right." He sighed. "Mother would be angry. She gave it to me as a birthday present." He put the violin down. I noticed how slim he was and how tall—above six feet—though his excessive leanness made him seem even taller. Now a marvellous brightness overtook his features. "You're the new boy," he said.

I offered my hand. "Yes, I have been transferred from another school. My name is—"

He interrupted me. "Wait, I will tell you."

I was puzzled. He began to study me in earnest. I started to feel uncomfortable. His perusal seemed to exude some invisible force. It was strong and penetrating. Satisfied with his efforts, he proceeded to address me.

"Your name is James Watson. You are from the north of England. Your father is a doctor. You spend a considerable amount of leisure time writing. And you have a particular fondness for custard tarts. Am I correct?"

I was, of course, dumbfounded yet slightly resentful that a perfect stranger should possess such intimate knowledge of me. Somewhat ungraciously I said, "My name isn't James. It is John." But it sounded rather carping.

"James . . . John . . . What's the difference?" he said peevishly.

"A great deal," I said with some force.

"Very well," he conceded. "Your name is John." But he was clearly anxious to know if he had been right, otherwise.

I could not withhold my admiration. "You were correct on every count." But I was dying to know how he had done it. "Is it some sort of magic?"

He beamed. "Not magic, Watson. Pure and simple deduction. First of all, please observe the name tag affixed to your mattress. It reads 'J. Watson.' So I selected what I considered to be a common name that begins with J. Although I opted for James, my second choice would have been John."

"Of course." I may have sounded dubious, but then he proceeded to dazzle me. "Your particular kind of shoes are not commonly worn in cities," he said. "They are a countryman's shoes of a kind I can recall having seen only once before when on a brief visit north. The skin of the middle finger of your left hand has a callus. That is often the trademark of a writer. And you have unpacked *Hunter's Encyclopedia of Disease.*"

"What of it?"

"Well, it is not a reference work available to the general public. However, it is in the libraries of medical schools and most practising physicians. Since someone of your age would not have been to a medical school, it must have been among the books possessed by someone close to you, someone concerned for your health while you are away from home. Someone very dear to you would have lent you that volume. Your father. A doctor?"

"Yes," I said. "And the custard tarts?"

"Simple. There is a distinct yellow stain on your left lapel. It is precisely the shade of yellow of the egg custard used in the making of custard tarts here in the south of England. And, well, your shape convinces me that you eat them frequently."

"There is no need to be rude," I said bluntly, but what might have built up in my mind as resentment of an uncalled-for insult (for so I considered it to be) was quickly diffused by the school bell.

"Come on, we haven't got all day," he said, snatching a textbook from his desk and beckoning me to follow.

"Where are you going?"

"To chemistry class, of course. Surely you don't want to miss that."

I could have pointed out that I had only just arrived, but his enthusiasm was infectious. "By the way," I said as we left the dormitory, "what is your name?"

"Holmes," he said. "Sherlock Holmes."

We crossed a medieval quadrangle from which cloisters and stone stairways issued clandestinely. Gas lamps glowed behind leaded windows, anticipating the winter twilight. It was a scene full of the ghosts of centuries. How many boys, I mused, must have crossed this courtyard before me, some destined to be leaders, others for failure, but most to lead average lives touched neither by greatness nor insupportable despair. In the centre stood a statue of the founder of the original school, that pious monarch fated to be murdered in the Tower. Beneath his effigy stood groups of boys, stamping their feet in the intense cold, their breath steamy in the frigid air.

But my new companion seemed quite impervious to

it. As we pressed on through the snow, he was lectur-
ing me on the subject of deduction.

"The deductive mind is never at rest, Watson," he
was saying. "It is not unlike a finely tuned musical
instrument. It demands constant attention and practise."

"And how does one go about fine tuning a mind?" I
must have sounded patronizing.

"With mathematical equations, problems of logic,
riddles. For example, you are seated in a room with an
all-southern view. A bear walks past the window.
What colour is the bear?"

"Red," I replied, considering this a ridiculously
simple conundrum. "The bear is red."

Holmes looked at me with disdain. "Why on earth
would the bear be red?"

"Because a southern sun is burning hot and the bear
would reflect its glow."

His expression was now one of incredulity. "That is
truly the most absurd answer I have ever heard. Who
said anything about a southern sun? I said a southern
view."

"Oh."

"You have got to think, Watson. Take your time.
Take the riddle apart. Study it piece by piece." He
shook his head despairingly. "Red!" he repeated in-
credulously. I felt I had been reduced to size.

We stomped our shoes before entering the chemistry room. The lecturer, a Mr. Snelgrove, was to arouse
the fear in me that if his performance were typical of
the general standard at Brompton, I would achieve an
education distinguished for its mediocrity. He was
senile; he had a face like a withered prune. He had a
habit of pausing in mid-sentence, staring into space,

and then, after what seemed an eternity, repeating the last word he had uttered, not just once but several times. "By combining the right amount of sodium potash . . . (long pause) . . . potash, yes potash, you will be able to complete the experiment . . . experiment . . . experiment," and so on. Sometimes he would drift into a vacancy so profound that only loud clearing of throats by students would bring him back to reality.

"How frightfully boring," I heard Holmes remark as the old man dithered with a tube of crystals which he poured into a phial of clear liquid; it turned a bright orange. We were now expected to repeat the experiment he had demonstrated, but Holmes disdained the opportunity, being content to watch me. At that moment we were distracted by a discreet tapping at a nearby window. A young girl pushed a note through a gap at its base and Holmes eagerly took it. I noted the amorous glance they exchanged and was surprised too that a girl, let alone one of such beauty, had access to the precincts of what I believed to be an all-male establishment. Naively I said: "Holmes, that was a girl!"

"Brilliant deduction," he said. I deserved his sarcasm. He unfolded the note.

"But who is she?" I asked. "What is she doing in a boys' school?"

"She lives here," he replied. "Her name is Elizabeth. Three years ago her parents died in a tragic accident in Philadelphia. So she came to live with her uncle, Professor Waxflatter, who used to teach here. When he retired, the school governors allowed him to keep his rooms. The professor became Elizabeth's guardian."

Holmes read the note and chuckled at its contents. He then handed it to me to read. It was a kind of poem. "What do you make of it?" he said.

I read the following verse:

> Two brains merge into one,
> Where the leaves of knowledge are stored
> Near the men of dancing words
> When the clock becomes a perfect *L*.

"It's gibberish," I said.

"On the contrary, Watson, it is a very clever message."

He explained the meaning of the note. "Elizabeth is saying that she would like to study with me or, as she puts it, she wants our two minds to merge into one. She wishes to meet me in the library 'where the leaves of knowledge are stored.' Books, my dear Watson, are leaves of knowledge. She wants to meet in the library 'near the men of dancing words.' She means, of course, the poetry section in the library. At exactly three o'clock."

"When the clock becomes a perfect *L*," I interjected.

"Very good, Watson," he said. Nevertheless, I considered it a pretentious way of communicating. However, Holmes was clearly delighted that she had taken so much trouble.

I had by now completed the experiment. My phial held a liquid, bright orange in colour.

"Bravo," said Holmes, patting me on the back indulgently, "but it is only a beginning."

Then, with the speed of light, he took the phial, held

it up, and winked at me. "Now for a bit of excitement," he said, and poured more chemicals into it.

The result was spectacular. The concoction bubbled and boiled. Sparks began to fly from it. They became balls of light, a fireworks display, until, in a marvellous finale, a burst of orange light lit up the entire laboratory! The students applauded. But Snelgrove was deeply disturbed. The vacuous old pedant was unlikely to forgive Holmes for this impertinent exhibition.

"We make a good team, Watson," said my companion. I was prepared to bask in his glory. "Come on, we shall be late getting to the library."

Indeed, we were late getting there, but this was entirely due to Holmes. He insisted that we stop first for a newspaper and then at an apothecary, where he purchased a bottle of cough syrup and took an ample swig from it. Then he said he knew a shortcut that would make up our lost time, but it turned out to be through an area where the school's incinerators disposed of the daily refuse. The heat from them had turned the snow into hardly navigable slush. Notwithstanding, Holmes blamed me for the delay and on reaching the library made a beeline for the poetry section. I noted his pleasure at finding Elizabeth still there and the opposite emotion when he realized that she was not alone. She was talking to a youth who obviously was flirting with her. Her beauty, I reflected, must have encouraged this. Living as she did among so many male adolescents, she must have been used to it. But this was not Holmes's reaction. He was at once hostile to the handsome youngster whose upper crust good looks and expensive clothes marked him as a son of rich parents. I later learned that Holmes and this boy, whose name was Dudley, were deadly rivals.

Dudley was showing Elizabeth a gold pocket watch of which he appeared inordinately proud. He was clearly hoping to impress her. "Elizabeth was admiring my new timepiece," he told Holmes. Holmes took it for closer inspection. "Stylish gentlemen are wearing them now," said Dudley foppishly.

"Expensive?"

"It came from an exclusive London jeweller."

Holmes was dubious. "I find that highly unlikely."

Dudley's temper rose. "I beg your pardon?"

"Had you taken a moment to examine your pocket watch," said Holmes, sounding excruciatingly patronizing, "you would have discovered that in style it is oriental. The face is Swiss, I grant you." He gave the watch a shake, as if expecting a rattle. "The movement is Italian. A complete mishmash. Your stylish timepiece is a fraud."

He could hardly have lit a more explosive fuse. Dudley snatched it back. "Keep your opinions to yourself, Holmes," he said with a hiss. To Elizabeth he bowed. He also kissed her hand and said: "I look forward to resuming our conversation." He turned pointedly to Holmes. "In circumstances of more privacy."

"Pompous ass," Holmes muttered as Dudley left.

"He is sweet," Elizabeth insisted.

"Is that why you allowed him to flirt with you?"

"I detect jealousy."

He denied this vigorously. "Sherlock Holmes jealous! The word is not in my vocabulary."

"Nor, it seems, is punctuality," Elizabeth retorted.

"Oh, I see. You were angry because I was late getting here. Well, I am sorry, but I can explain. You see, after leaving chemistry class . . ."

"Wait, Holmes. Let me." She wanted to play his deduction game. "Following chemistry class, you ran to the newspaper shop to buy a copy of *The Times*. Then you made a dash to the apothecary to pick up your cough medicine. Upon realizing you were late you took the shortcut."

"Very good," said Holmes.

"Quite simple really," said Elizabeth. "Your finger-tips are stained with newspaper ink. Your breath smells of licorice and codeine. And your shoes are sprinkled with mud. The only muddy path in this cold weather is the one near the incinerators."

"I've taught you well," said Holmes.

"I've taught *you* well," she replied.

They kissed tenderly and I felt I should leave them to themselves. Besides, I was anxious to explore the library.

Its musty smell suggested that slumbering in its darker recesses were volumes that had remained readerless for years. I made for the history shelves. Pausing at the *E–H* section I spotted a copy of Herodotus in such a rich antique binding that I felt compelled to handle it. But it was at an unreachable height.

I climbed a set of conventionally placed steps to withdraw the volume. I was on the point of so doing when my ears were assailed by a jingling sound. It was coming from someone simultaneously ascending a stepladder at the opposite side of the shelf. As I withdrew Herodotus, I became aware that the producer of the sound was about to take out a volume from a corresponding position on his side. Through the gap I would be able to see the jingler, but this was not to be.

Never good on steps, I lost my footing. I fell, landing amid a shower of books, including Herodotus, on the floor. *Thump!* In the disturbance the jingler fled.

Elizabeth and Holmes came to my aid. They helped me to my feet. "Elizabeth," said Holmes, "I would like you to meet my new friend, the honorable but clumsy Watson."

Of course, I considered the introduction untimely and not at all well phrased, but I contained my feeling. Elizabeth was quick to put me at ease. The sincerity in her lovely eyes was balm to my frayed dignity. I had made another friend. And I had quite forgotten about Herodotus.

When fully recovered I joined my companions in a stroll across the quadrangle. I felt at ease with them for although I had sensed that the relationship between Holmes and Elizabeth was special, her nature was such as not to exclude me. Her grace and poise amounted to something very rare. I recalled what Holmes had told me, that she had a tragic history, and I suspected that her early maturity stemmed from suffering. Losses such as she had experienced tend to make or break us; in her case it had fashioned an understanding beyond her years.

My reflections were cut short by a voice crying, "Holmes! Elizabeth!" We looked in the direction from whence the voice had come. This proved to be a rooftop from which a most extraordinary-looking fellow was waving to us. From his snowy white hair and abundant grey beard I judged him to be well into his seventies, but the agility of his manner belied his age. His dress was eccentric too, for he had on a bright

34

jersey and knickerbockers held up by braces. Atop his mop of hair, a tweed cap of unusual design perched at a crazily cockeyed angle. He was the oddest-looking party I had ever clapped eyes on. "I think I have solved all the problems, Holmes," he called, immediately dashing across the roof and out of sight.

"Who is that?" I asked in astonishment.

"My uncle," said Elizabeth.

Holmes elaborated. "Rupert T. Waxflatter, science professor, now retired. He holds degrees in chemistry and biology, is well versed in philosophy, mathematics, and physics, and is the author of no less than twenty-seven learned works."

"Amazing."

"And most people think he is a lunatic," added Elizabeth.

"Why?" I asked out of politeness, for I considered him to be as mad as a hatter. What happened next surely confirmed it. The old boy was hauling along a ramp a bizarre mechanical contraption equipped with translucent wings. It looked like a monstrous insect, but on further consideration I realized it was some sort of flying machine. It bore some resemblance to a realization of plans for a flying machine which Leonardo da Vinci had incorporated in his famous notebooks. The professor strapped himself in, pulled a lever on the ramp, and shot into the air. Moreover, the contraption actually flew! At its helm the old man was pedalling furiously. But in only a matter of moments, the wings began to sag, and the machine went into a glide. Its flight took on a perilous, twirling pattern. It was clearly going to crash. Crash it did, disintegrating amid trees, hurling the professor to rest in a cradle of the leafless branches of one of them.

We hurried to the scene. The tree had saved the professor, but the machine was a wreck. At this juncture a stranger appeared from one of the arcane alleys that threaded the school building. He was an elderly, unkempt person with a stubble of beard and nervous, fugitive eyes. He took one appalled glance at the mishap and left as quickly as he had appeared. Meanwhile, we had reached Waxflatter and were extricating him. He was unscathed. He expressed concern only for his machine. "That makes six," he grumbled. "Six failed attempts." We gathered up the bits and laboriously climbed the several flights of stairs which led to the professor's abode.

This turned out to be an enormous attic, which he had converted into a laboratory of sorts. It was more like a scientific junkyard, a cornucopia of ideas half-realized, though one at least, an immense brass chronometer, was capable of impulsive motion. It startled me out of my wits! Everywhere there were books open for consultation, maps of the world and the heavens, and models in different stages of evolution of the machine we had just seen crash. This workshop-cum-living quarters reflected a probing mind and restless heart. Although stuffed with papers and books, it was in no way claustrophobic because it was wrapped around with windows affording marvellous panoramic views of London. One of them gave me my first sight of the Palace of Westminster and Big Ben.

"I live here with Uncle," Elizabeth was informing me as if that were the most natural thing in the world. "When he retired the school let him keep his attic. They wanted his work to continue."

"Of course." I said it with little conviction because it seemed to me the dotty old fellow never completed anything. The attic was a museum of what might have been. But Holmes was enthusiastic. "I've spent many happy hours here," he said. "The professor has taught me more than ten other masters put together." I then realized that a dog was also present, a Jack Russell terrier of diminutive stature and much vitality. It was licking my ankle. "Say hello to Watson, Uncas," said Elizabeth. Uncas did and I further encouraged his attention by providing him with a caramel from a supply purchased that morning at Euston Station. I reminded myself that it was only hours ago, for it seemed a lifetime. Here I was on my first day at a new school, in the company of Holmes, Elizabeth, a lovable little dog, and a potty inventor!

The old man was sifting through parts of the disintegrated machine, examining each with a magnifying glass. He was trying to detect faults. "Have you found the weakness, sir?" asked Holmes respectfully.

"Oh, I foolishly constructed the wings out of an inferior material. They must be strengthened. I shall have to rebuild the entire machine again."

"The entire machine? Won't that be difficult?"

Waxflatter shrugged. "Elementary, my dear Holmes," he replied. "Elementary." It was a phrase I was to hear repeated many times over the years. Judging from Holmes's and Elizabeth's smiles, they too had heard it before. One could not help but be indulgent; the old fellow had such indomitable spirit.

But at that moment the door of the attic noisily opened. Framed there was a man I recognized as the mysterious stranger who had appeared briefly in the schoolyard. He held a newspaper in one hand. The effect upon the professor was traumatic. He went quite pale. Tieing Uncas to a leash, he turned to

Elizabeth. "You'll have to excuse me," he said. "Why not take little Uncas for a walk?"

Elizabeth took the leash. With nervous haste the old man ushered us out. As we passed I saw Holmes look at the mysterious caller's newspaper. One item in it stood out because it had been circled in pencil. It read as follows: "London Accountant Bentley Bobster Commits Suicide." We heard the attic door bolted behind us.

Puzzled yet silent, we walked back across the yard. None of us wished to theorize. Holmes's mind was working furiously. His concentration was like a tangible force. Yet I had no wish to question him prematurely. To be perfectly frank, I was anxious only for a good night's sleep. It had been a most eventful day.

Chapter Three

I AWOKE THE NEXT MORNING CONVINCED THAT I HAD
the answer. Not to the identity of Waxflatter's unexpected guest but to the riddle Holmes had set me.
Holmes was then an early riser, a characteristic he
would not maintain through life, so I rushed over to
the gymnasium to inform him. "I've got it, Holmes," I
gushed.

"Got what, old fellow?" He was not in the least
receptive.

"The solution to the riddle, Holmes. The bear is
black."

This irritated him. "Wrong again, Watson. The bear
is not black. And I would appreciate it if you would not
disturb me while I am trying to concentrate on a
fencing lesson."

The gymnasium was the great hall of the building
and it dated back to the fifteenth century. Its lofty
ceilings were covered in grotesque oak carvings
which, with the tall, decorated windows and huge
central hearth, testified to a rich past. It was already

two hundred years old when Henry VIII visited to feast "with much magnificence" as the guest of an influential duke. One hundred years later, Queen Elizabeth put in an appearance for a secret rendezvous with the handsome earl of Essex.

All the boys were present in the gymnasium that morning, and except for Holmes and myself, they were engaged in desultory practise with the foil. It did not take me long to observe that the standard of prowess was unexceptional. It was their instructor, William Rathe, who impressed me. This lithe, pantherish person, clearly in peak condition and all of six feet tall, dominated the proceedings. When he demonstrated a move, one could not help but admire his suppleness, the coordination of his body. His skin was firm and bronzed as if by a southern sun or mountain air. His brown hair, dark eyes, and high cheekbones suggested Mediterranean origins, Italian perhaps, but if I had had to guess, I would have placed them somewhere even more southerly. I judged him to be about forty. Holmes was watching this interesting fellow intently.

Rathe was fencing with a student who plainly lacked confidence, and one sensed that the instructor felt the lack of a more inspired partner. Inevitably, the boy made a careless move, lost his balance, and fell awkwardly onto the bare stone floor. The pain he was experiencing suggested he had twisted an ankle. Rathe helped him to his feet and led him to the school matron, who seated the limping boy and began examining the sprain. Mrs. Dribb was as motherly a figure as any school might wish for a matron. She wore the uniform of a nurse on a fulsome body. Her hair was done up in a bun and she had a kindly countenance. Rathe returned to the class.

"Remember, gentlemen," he began. "We cannot allow ourselves lapses of concentration. We must work on technique and rhythm and balance."

"Yes, Mr. Rathe," the students replied in unison.

"I can think of no better pupil to help me illustrate the proper form and technique," he said, snapping his fingers at Holmes, "than young Mr. Sherlock Holmes."

Holmes sprang to his feet, donned a mask, and crossed to the centre of the floor. I looked at Dudley. His reaction was one of intense jealousy.

"Study our stance, our movements, our style," Rathe continued. Then he lowered his mask and exchanged a ritual nod of chivalry with Holmes. They then crossed foils.

"En garde!"

In contrast to what I had previously seen, this duel was inspired. Despite the difference in their ages, Rathe and Holmes were keenly matched, for what advantage the instructor possessed in experience and technique his pupil made up for in youthful energy and verve. Even Mrs. Dribb looked up from her bandaging. The match had become impassioned, more competitive and heated than a mere demonstration should have been. All eyes were on the two men, each of whom was determined to outmatch the other. Everyone present was riveted by the splendid display— except for Dudley, who could not conceal his envy. Then Holmes made a sudden lunge, Rathe parried it, and Holmes slid to the ground, his foil flying out of his hand. Quick as lightning Rathe moved the tip of his blade to Holmes's throat. "*Touché!* My game!" he exclaimed.

The protagonists removed their masks, Holmes breathing hard, Rathe perfectly composed. They shook hands. "Holmes lost because of one important factor," Rathe told the class. "His emotions took over. He ignored discipline." To Holmes he emphasized the point. "Never let discipline be replaced with emotion," he said. Then he ruffled Holmes's hair in a friendly gesture. "Good show, Holmes," he said.

For the rest of the day I was occupied with registering for the particular courses I would myself be taking during the two years I had to spend at Brompton. I would concentrate on subjects which would best prepare me for medical studies at university, for, as I have said, I aspired to become a doctor. So I saw little of Holmes until we met in the dining hall. There, by candlelight, the student body had assembled. At High Table was the entire teaching faculty. As a group they were most dispiriting. Their advanced ages and sour faces were evidence that the years they had spent in that institution had divested their countenances of every shred of humour. Schools like Brompton, I reflected, were islands. They were remote from the cut and thrust of the human condition. Here we were at the centre of the greatest city on earth, yet we might as well have been on the moon. We were entirely screened from reality. Wisdom, it has always seemed to me, is not a mere concomitant of the passage of time, as these grim-faced academics arrayed before us no doubt believed it to be; it comes from the sorrows and delights of human relationships. Enclose a man for his entire working life in an educational cell and he becomes institutionalized, introverted, dull. Even the padre, muttering an almost inaudible prayer in Latin from High Table, seemed to have found nothing in godliness to gladden him. His solemnity did nothing to lift our spirits. There was one exception in this sad company—only Rathe projected a friendly sense of being one of us.

We were seated at the back of the hall. Holmes studiously ignored prayers. Above his soup plate rested a book (it was a volume of the da Vinci notebooks) and he was absorbed in it. Also at our table were Dudley and a spotty youth named Jeremy. With us was a nearsighted, pasty-faced fellow called Colin and a big-bodied one called Henry, who had gained a reputation as an athlete.

While waiting for the soup to be served, our conversation revolved around our ambitions for future careers. Dudley had no doubt about his: he would become an army general. "Generals don't make money," said Colin, much to Dudley's annoyance. Jeremy said he would prefer to be a writer. Colin again volunteered the opinion that writers don't make money either. Then Henry said he wanted to be a barrister. "Ah yes," said Colin. "Barristers make money." Obviously, Colin himself simply wanted to make money, and the conversation might have dried up there, had not Dudley been intent on drawing Holmes into it. "What about you, Holmes?" said Dudley. "What do you want to be when you grow up?"

Holmes looked up slowly from his book, but he did not immediately reply. Feeling a bit left out, I interjected: "I want to be a doctor." Half expecting Colin to say that doctors don't make money, I was all the more surprised—and annoyed—by Dudley's quite un-called-for rudeness. "Nobody asked you," he snapped. By which time Holmes was ready with his reply, influenced, I suspected, by having caught sight of Elizabeth walking her dog.

"I never want to be alone," he said. The boys looked puzzled; it had gone right above their heads. Soup arrived and we settled down to it in silence. It was a lentil soup, not at all bad, but to my regret second helpings were out of the question.

After dinner Holmes went to look for Elizabeth in the school gardens. She told him of an unnerving experience she had had while walking Uncas that evening. Someone, mysteriously swathed in a cloak, had crossed the courtyard. Whoever it was had emitted what she described as "little bells jingling." Uncas had given chase. The intruder had managed to scramble over a wall, but not before the plucky little terrier had wrenched off a bit of the black cloak which the wearer positively refused to give up. Much later, when Holmes related this to me, I was reminded of my experience in the library the previous day, but I cannot say he reacted with any great show of interest when I gave him this information. He simply took it in. I might just as well have confided it to one of those phonograph machines which had recently so impressed the Royal Association. Somehow, I assumed, he was storing it up for later processing in his deductive mind. For myself I could not help but wonder who it was that Uncas had chased and upon what mission he was bound. For Holmes and myself the answer to that question lay in the future. However, for the Reverend Duncan Nesbit, vicar of St. Cyprian's in the suburb of Kilburn, it was to come much sooner.

Evensong in the gauntly Gothic-style church was over. All that remained for the elderly priest to do was to extinguish the altar candles and those beside the offertory box. Then he would close the church door and lock it. In the vicarage his housekeeper would have placed his slippers to warm beside a banked-up fire. Closing the church after evensong was a chore he usually delegated to the curate, but he had given his young associate permission to attend a lantern lecture. The subject of it was the leper colonies of Fiji, an interest in which he had no wish to discourage him.

A kindly man, bent slightly now, the Reverend Duncan Nesbit went about his business in the darkening church. Its majestic organ and glorious stained glass were symbols of which he was proud. They represented the growing prosperity of his congregation and, of course, their piety, for Kilburn was expanding with rows of fine four-storied houses for the families of professional men who daily took trains to the city. He sighed contentedly. The Lord had been good to him, not merely in granting him this parish but in giving him so devout and respectable a congregation. Would he be presumptuous in believing that it was a reward for his undiminished faith?

It was a faith that had undergone one exceptional trial. For, prior to his decision to take holy orders, he had had to wrestle with the demands of the flesh. It took place in a period between his schooling at Old Broms and his studies for the ministry. He had taken the opportunity of the interim to travel, joining a group of contemporaries from his old school in a venture that took them to lands where other gods were worshipped. Of course, he realized later that such people were misguided heathens, but, being young, he had for a period accepted the philosophical view that religion, being man-made, was bound to be as various as mankind itself. It was a radical outlook, which a relationship he had formed in a Moslem country had not helped him to dispel. He had fallen in love.

She was the daughter of an Egyptian cotton-grower, and they had met while he was on a visit to provincial Zagazig in the Egyptian delta. How he had wrestled with his spirit! Of course, he realized later that it was his essential Englishness that had saved him—and some wise letters from his parents, who had pointed out how out of place an Arabic girl would feel in Harrogate, the family home, and how unsettling her presence would be to the unwed ladies of that respectable spa. Finally, he had renounced his intention of marrying. To the relief of family and friends, he had returned home to prepare for the priesthood. He had never married. After ordination he had been called to St. Cyprian's, where he had been for over thirty years, respected and, he believed, appreciated.

There was always consolation to be derived from sacrifice, the Reverend Nesbit told himself, if indeed a sacrifice was what he had made. As he prepared to quench the last altar candle he felt at peace with the past.

He moved to those candles that still flickered beside the offertory, stopping to admire for the umpteenth time the stained-glass window he loved most. It was a portrayal in scarlet and yellow and blue of the young Judas accepting the thirty pieces of silver. Over the years it had been a constant reminder to him of the greed of man and Satan's power to divert him from his rightful calling.

Just then he heard a musical sound, a sort of jingling, and he felt a sudden stab of pain. He discounted the jingling as an abberation. He thought little of the pain; it had lasted only a split-second. But the trusting priest had not seen a cloaked figure lower a blowpipe and leave through the open door. He was still looking appreciatively at the craftsmanship that had gone into the depiction of Judas's act of betrayal.

Then the unbelievable happened. The Roman soldier in the picture came to life! He leapt from the window and stood in the aisle. Though shocked, the priest also felt a glow of elation. Surely he was in the presence of a miracle. Only when the soldier drew his sword and moved menacingly toward him did fear overtake the gentle cleric. This was the Devil's ingenuity. He let forth a quite inhuman scream.

The soldier came closer, brandishing the terrible weapon, and the old man bolted. He put every ounce of his strength into the effort to escape. Gathering up his priestly robes he ran to the open door and dashed blindly down the steps to the busy street. Across it lay the vicarage. He had to get there.

It was a carriage, a four-wheeler travelling at top speed, that hit him. The crazed priest ran straight into the path of the horses. A crowd gathered, but nothing could be done. When they extricated him it was clear that he was dead, a fact also noted by a cloaked figure.

Inside St. Cyprian's a solitary candle still flickered. In the stillness, Judas and the soldier stood transfixed. The depiction of their regrettable transaction was as it had always been, ever since the church's consecration.

Chapter Four

MY FASCINATION WITH THE CHARACTER OF SHER-
lock Holmes increased with each day. I can honestly
say that hero-worship was not an ingredient of it.
Between adolescents thrust into each other's company, such feelings can easily develop and, in the
introverted atmosphere of an English public school,
become unhealthy. No, it was the mind of Holmes and
the way he used it that intrigued me. His powers of
analytical deduction were so remarkable—my one regret was that the superiority over his fellows which it
afforded him sometimes expressed itself in intolerance
of them. It would be too strong to call Holmes arro-
gant. It was simply that he saw things differently from
the common man.

Mind you, there were aspects of his personality of
which I was strongly critical, although I refrained from
voicing my feelings. I believed then, as I do now, that
one accepts a man, warts and all, and that if the sum of
his faults is more than the sum of his appeal, you step
aside. Judge not lest you be judged is an aphorism to

which I have tried to adhere. We are ill-equipped to judge our fellows. As Holmes once pointed out to me (and which I related in "The Sign of Four"), it is of the first importance not to allow one's judgment to be biased by personal qualities. The most winning woman he had ever known, he once told me, was hanged for poisoning three little children for their insurance money, while the most repellent man of his acquaintance had been a philanthropist who had spent a quarter of a million on the London poor.

So it may seem petty to mention some of Holmes's less-endearing qualities, such as his ability to become bored and incommunicative if there was not at the time some drama or excitement to concentrate his thoughts upon. It was at such times that he retreated into a corner and endeavoured to play his violin, which in fairness I must say he became more proficient with as the years went by. He could be uncomfortably moody. There was egotism too, which permitted him to be contemptuous of areas of human knowledge about which he was totally ignorant. Much later in our friendship I was to make a list of his capacities in various subjects. For example, his knowledge of literature, except where it centered upon sensation or crime, was almost nil. Sometimes, of course, sensation is treated in a literary way—as in the work of Poe—yet when once I paid him what I considered to be a compliment by comparing his powers with those of Poe's detective Dupin, he countered with a shrug. Dupin was a very inferior fellow, he said. Philosophy and astronomy did not concern Holmes. He was quite feeble on the subject of politics. His knowledge of botany was inexact. He knew nothing about plants yet all about poisons. He was only marginally interested in non-human species and could dissect a dog as easily as pat it if the result promised to be to his analytical advantage. His knowledge of chemistry was profound; of anatomy, accurate; and of English law, very practical. Even in these student years he was developing some very odd interests, such as in the composition of soils, the varieties of cigar and cigarette ash, and in footprints. An extremely annoying characteristic, however, was his ability to condemn as a waste of time areas of knowledge which most of us consider essential and important. Many years after our school days, I was to write that he was in total ignorance, or feigned to be, of the workings of the solar system. For all he cared, the earth might have been flat. "You appear to be astonished that I didn't know," he said when I explained to him the Copernican theory. "Well, now that I know I shall do my best to forget about it. It is of the highest importance not to allow useless facts to elbow out the useful ones."

"But the solar system!" I exclaimed.

"What the deuce is it to me? You say we go 'round the sun. If we went 'round the moon it would not make a penny's worth of difference to me or my work."

But what exactly was his work, what was he aspiring to be? I asked myself that question many times during our time at Brompton. It was only a respectful wish not to pry that inhibited me from directly questioning him on the subject.

Yet he appeared to be obsessed with reports of crime, of which London was a veritable cesspool, and possessed knowledge of every horror perpetuated in our century. Looking back, I suppose that had I been more perceptive, I would have realized that Holmes's future lay in that area. But would I have foreseen the end result, that Sherlock Holmes was destined to become the most distinguished consulting detective the world has ever known, an amateur sleuth whose powers of observation, perception, and deduction would earn him the respect and envy of Scotland Yard? I think not. We were, after all, only schoolboys.

Even Holmes, with his formidable intelligence, was not immune to joining in schoolboy pranks. Indeed, it was at the beginning of my second week at Brompton that he showed a special zest for one. The entire school was bursting with excitement. Dudley had challenged Holmes to a test of ingenuity and deduction. He had purloined the school fencing trophy and hidden it. Holmes had to discover the trophy's secret hiding place within sixty minutes. Dudley would time him with a stopwatch. Holmes accepted the challenge and with a confident glance at Elizabeth, cried, "The game is afoot!"

Holmes started off across the quadrangle, followed at a discreet distance by the boys. Most masters were present, too. Rathe, in particular, was rooting for him. Waxflatter had gone up to his roof to wave encouragement. Only Snelgrove disapproved; he thought the contest undignified and a waste of valuable school time. Yet there was no disputing that the rest of us had caught the spirit of the challenge and wanted Holmes to succeed.

His quest took him to the art department, where he closely scrutinized the tubes of colour in Dudley's paintbox, though we knew not why. Holmes had told me that in deduction he reasoned backwards, from result back to cause, so I suppose at the outset he had a theory in his mind and hoped that future discovery would bear it out. Anyway, he returned to the quadrangle and began to follow footprints in the snow, which led to the science lab where, in passing, he appraised a skeleton used in anatomical studies, but on observing a crack beneath a window, he opened it and climbed out. He reached the fire escape and ascended to the roof. Crossing the building he came to a gap of some ten feet between it and the adjacent one, which was the refectory. To everyone's astonishment he took a running leap and jumped the gap, only just making it. Then he disappeared through a skylight.

"Despicable," I overheard Snelgrove complain. "A student acting like a chimpanzee." But Mrs. Dribb reproached him. "Now, Mr. Snelgrove, he's just having a bit of fun. Surely you can remember what fun is about."

"Bah!" retorted Snelgrove. "That boy is too precocious and egotistical for his own good. He'll never find that trophy."

"I'll wager you one guinea that he does," said Rathe, and the chemistry master accepted.

Once inside the kitchen of the refectory, Holmes began searching cupboards and shelves. He even examined pots and pans. Surely he didn't expect the trophy to be among them. No. He was looking for something else, something he found beneath an oven. There lay some white particles, which he proceeded to examine with a magnifying glass. Then he was off again, but as he crossed the courtyard his confidence appeared to sag. He looked quite baffled, so much so that we all felt Holmes was going to fail.

I checked my watch and called to him, "You've only got five minutes, Holmes." He appeared not to hear, so I called again.

"I heard you the first time," he snapped. "Can't you see I'm trying to concentrate?"

Well, I suppose I should have known better. But I was convinced that he had lost. To pacify myself, I devoured a caramel. As he walked back to the main building I could see a veil of disappointment cover his features. He was going to give up; of this I was certain. He made for the central staircase and stomped his snow-caked boots on the first step. He looked down at his boots, now revealed amid a circle of crumbled snow, and his face lit up. He bounded up the rest of the stairs two at a time. On reaching the main lobby he faced the great fireplace beside which Dudley was holding his stopwatch. "Two minutes left, Holmes," said Babcock. "I assume you are giving up."

"Never assume anything, my good fellow."

"But I see no sign of the trophy, Holmes."

"But I do."

Triumphantly, Holmes reached to the mantel and took down a large, richly coloured vase. He was on the point of dashing it to the floor when Snelgrove ran forward. "Holmes! Have you gone mad? This is an antique!" But Holmes was not to be deterred. Before anyone could stop him he had flung it down. It disintegrated into small pieces revealing, amid the debris, the school fencing trophy!

It was an heroic moment. Amid the excitement I saw Snelgrove ill-humouredly hand a golden guinea to Rathe. Dudley left, seething with venomous hostility. But the crowd cheered and Elizabeth and I beamed with pleasure.

In the dormitory later that day I asked Holmes for an explanation. He was in a mood of impenetrable reserve, playing his violin with a little less discordance than usual, and I was by no means sure he would reply. But he rested the instrument and did so.

"In the kitchen beneath the oven I noticed particles of freshly baked ceramic," he began. "I thought that odd in a kitchen used only for the preparation of food. I remembered Dudley's paintbox. The colours in it had obviously recently been used. But nothing came together until I was crossing the courtyard, and I began to think of footprints. You may recall that when I reached the stairs I scuffed my feet to shake off the impacted snow. The snow crumbled around my boots in an even pile. It was that image which struck a chord, a parallel between my foot encased in snow and the trophy encased in a vase. The only vase I could bring to mind was the precious antique above the lobby fireplace. But, of course, Dudley would not have dared to tamper with that. He would have had to make a replica. But he made such a bad job of it that I knew at once it was an imitation. I dashed it to pieces and, of course, revealed the trophy."

"Amazing, Holmes. Truly amazing."

At which point we were distracted by a voice beyond the window. "Holmes!" Waxflatter was calling urgently. He was on the roof again. A new version of his flying machine stood perilously at the edge. The wings were larger and the figure "7" had been painted on the fuselage.

"This time I've definitely solved the problem," the dotty old fellow exclaimed. He strapped himself in and pulled the lever. Within seconds he was soaring above us. But not for long. He was having difficulty navigating. The controls were refusing to respond. Flying machine number seven was in rapid descent. It glided toward a snowdrift, landing in it with a certain dignity. Holmes and I started off to pick up the pieces.

Later, in Waxflatter's attic, the professor appeared none the worse for his ordeal and we placed the various components in a heap. We were about to leave him to his research when I saw Holmes pause at Waxflatter's desk. On it lay a newspaper opened to the obituary section. An article had been circled in pencil. The heading read: "Reverend Duncan Nesbit Trampled to Death." Holmes read the article through and looked troubled. If his glance at Waxflatter was anything to go by, his main anxiety was for the professor.

During the noonday break a few days later, Holmes invited me to accompany him to the headquarters of the metropolitan police. I was startled by his invitation though nonetheless complimented that he should value my moral support. A protected upbringing had not equipped me for contact with the enforcers of the law. The job of the police was to protect property and, so far as they could, human life, but I had always been encouraged to believe that involvement with them was best avoided.

I knew that something weighty had been oppressing Holmes; the dormitory had been treated to more than its fair share of his performances on the violin. I assumed that the mission upon which he intended to embark was connected with whatever it was that engrossed him. But it did come as a surprise to me to learn that he was no stranger to the corridors of the police establishment at New Scotland Yard on the

Victoria Embankment. He knew his way about very well and located with ease the office of the official he had come to see.

"Holmes!" exclaimed this officer. He was clearly dismayed by the intrusion. "It has been a long time since your last visit. Three or four days?" But the sarcasm was lost on Holmes.

"This will only take a minute of your time, Mr. Lestrade," he said.

The rank of the policeman was detective-sergeant. This was discernible from a brass nameplate on his desk. The fact that Holmes did not use it when addressing him did nothing to improve the atmosphere.

The podgy, balding young policeman had a sallow complexion and a smudge of a moustache. He bristled with self-importance. He was, I reckoned, in his mid-twenties. I conjectured that he lived in one of the new estates being built in Camberwell or such other southern suburb. He probably had a sweet little wife, ambitious for him to climb still further up the constabulary ladder. Most definitely, he regarded Holmes as an interfering, over-educated young pipsqueak bent on wasting his time.

Public schoolboys in England are passively thought of by the general public as privileged. Lestrade, however, represented the new lower middle-class. No doubt he resented Holmes for the education he had not himself had the fortune to receive. To get where he was, which was behind piles of paperwork at an unimposing desk, he had worked hard.

"There are no new murder reports for you to study, Holmes, no casebooks you haven't read," said the harassed policeman. He regretted ever having allowed this irritating youth into headquarters. He recalled the first occasion when Holmes had knocked on his office door and explained that he was writing a thesis on crime which would be considerably assisted by contact with a working detective. Why had he agreed? Lestrade wondered. Had he felt flattered? Had he mistakenly believed that to assist a boy from the Brompton School would stand him in good stead with his superiors? Whatever his motive had been, he utterly regretted it.

He patted the documents on his desk impatiently. "Well, Holmes?"

"I am not here for research reasons," Holmes said blandly. "You see, I believe I am onto something."

"Not again!" said Lestrade.

"This time I am certain of it."

The policeman again resorted to sarcasm. "Really," he said. "Just like last month when you were convinced that the French ambassador was embezzling three hundred thousand pounds?"

"I was close," said Holmes. "It turned out to be the Russian ambassador."

"Holmes, I really don't have the time for your playpen theories."

Holmes displayed two newspaper clippings. They were accounts of the deaths of Bobster and Nesbit. He handed them to the detective. "Just have a quick look at these. I suspect foul play," said Holmes.

"But these incidents are completely unrelated."

"Wrong. Both men graduated from the same university in the same year."

"Coincidence," said Lestrade.

Holmes took back his clippings. "Neither of their deaths fit their personalities," he said. "According to this account, Bobster was a happy man, content with life, his career, his family. Why should he commit suicide? He didn't even leave a note." He waited in vain for Lestrade to react. "And the Reverend Nesbit has been described by his friends as 'warm, loving, peaceful,' the newspaper says. Yet the driver of the carriage saw him as 'insane, crazed, and in a state of panic' when he ran into the path of the horses."

Lestrade considered this briefly. He became patronizing. "A fluctuation of character, Holmes, is hardly evidence with which to begin an investigation." Then impatience returned. "My advice to you is to keep your nose out of the newspapers and in your schoolbooks."

Holmes sighed, aware that he was getting nowhere. "I appreciate your time, Mr. Lestrade," he said, handing the clippings to the detective again. "I suggest you hold on to these. You know, if I were a detective-sergeant, trapped in this room by boring paperwork, I would be doing all in my power to find that one case, that one promising investigation that could earn me promotion to inspector." With this he indicated that we were leaving.

As I closed the door, I saw Lestrade, puffed with indignation, pick up the clippings and begin to read.

Two weeks before Christmas we sat the end-of-term examination. I felt reasonably confident. My transfer from a previous school to Old Broms could easily have been to my disadvantage, but it had had the opposite effect. So far as the curriculum was concerned, the class I had joined was at least a term behind the one I had left. I wanted to do well. A good record at Brompton would help me achieve a university place, which was vital to my medical studies. For his part, Holmes was indifferent to the exams, though everyone expected him to do well; his record of achievement was the best in the school. He was also contemptuous of the examination method. Success in exams, he maintained, was no proof of intelligence. It was like asking a bricklayer to make bricks. Intelligence lay in the craftsmanship of laying them. Nevertheless, he was obliged to sit the exam.

No talking was allowed in the examination room. Holmes was at a desk between mine and Dudley's. Snelgrove handed out the papers. After the ordeal began, I saw Dudley drop a document on the floor. Holmes noticed it too, picked it up, and was about to return it to Dudley when Snelgrove spotted him.

"What are you doing, Holmes?" he demanded.

"Dudley dropped this, sir," Holmes explained. "I was about to give it back to him."

Dudley feigned surprise.

"It's your paper, Dudley," said Holmes.

"It doesn't belong to me," came the reply.

"But you dropped it," Holmes insisted.

Dudley looked at the document. "It is not even in my handwriting."

Holmes now scrutinized it closely. He was in for a shock. The handwriting was an excellent forgery of his own. But he was given no time to object because Snelgrove grabbed the document and read it.

"Well, Holmes," said the master with unmistakable satisfaction, "it appears that we have finally discovered the secret of your brilliance. These are the answers to the examination questions."

Dudley was a picture of innocence. Snelgrove pocketed the document and took Holmes by the collar. "You had better come with me," he said. Utterly confused, Holmes was led from the room. Dudley gloated. It would have been useless to attempt to defend Holmes. Snelgrove had him in his power, something he had wished for ever since the display of pyrotechnics in the chemistry class.

"Honesty, Probity, Diligence"—that was the school motto, and Holmes had offended every tenet of it. Or so the governors decided when they met to decide his future. In their darkly panelled room, the motto was above the mantel, lettered in gold in a carved yew frame—in Latin, of course. For someone who had so flagrantly flaunted its values, there was no future at all at Brompton. Only Rathe defended him, spiritedly reminding the cadre of old men that Holmes was an outstanding student with a level of intelligence rare in a boy of his age. But the governors were not moved. Indeed, as Snelgrove pointed out, Holmes's brilliant term reports and high marks suggested that he had been cheating from the moment he had joined the school. So the more Rathe spoke of Holmes's achievements, the more the craggy faces expressed certainty that Holmes was guilty and must go. They decided to expel him. All this was reported to Holmes by Rathe. Holmes told me later that the fencing instructor was so incensed by the unfairness of the decision that he had offered to write him a sterling recommendation to any other school to which he might apply. "Is there anything else I can do?" Rathe had asked in conclusion. To this Holmes replied with a request for a final friendly duel of swordsmanship with the instructor. Rathe at once agreed and I alone was privileged to witness the encounter in an otherwise empty gymnasium.

It was like watching dancers, so balletic was the effect of their thrusts and parries. Neither man wore a mask or protective clothing; the match had been hastily arranged. Obviously they completely trusted each other's control. But an unfortunate thing happened. A ring Rathe was wearing bore an emblem which glinted and dazzled Holmes. At a moment when Rathe's foil was on the point of contact, Holmes froze, as if hypnotized. Rathe tried to change direction. In doing so, the hand which bore the ring grazed Holmes' cheek, the sharp edge of the emblem cutting it deeply. "Just a small cut," Holmes said, but he was bleeding profusely. "I lost my concentration."

"It was the ring," said Rathe. "I should have removed it. The glint from it gave me an unfair advantage. The match is yours."

"Shall we call it a draw?"

They shook hands. "I will never forget you, sir," Holmes said sadly. "I could not have wished for a better instructor."

"Nor I a better student. And I am sure our foils will cross again."

Rathe and Mrs. Dribb walked Holmes to the matron's office. With motherly care she cleansed his cut and applied a plaster patch. Obviously this kindly woman had much affection for her boys. When she had done her work she drew him close and gave him a gentle kiss. "We are all going to miss you, Mr. Holmes," she said. He was grateful. He had made another friend, and he bowed to her.

Someone else, of course, would miss Holmes. That evening Elizabeth met him in the courtyard. Holmes confided to me the following day that he had realized at their meeting how much he loved Elizabeth. She had assured him of her love too. Although they were both very young, they had no doubt at all that their love was unique and permanent. They had declared this to one another. And, of course, it is often the case that a first love is the truest of all. It is sometimes the only true love we ever know.

For my part, I was determined that Holmes should be avenged. I wanted to give Dudley a good hiding, but his physique was superior to my own. I pledged myself to take boxing lessons.

Holmes knew I was upset. "Now, Watson, don't be emotional," he advised. "Revenge is sweeter when served with a smile."

I was not to realize his implications until later. We were crossing the central lobby, transporting Holmes's portmanteau and violin case to the main gate, when Dudley ran toward us screaming. His hair was as white as snow!

"You did this to me, Holmes, you fiend," he cried.

"It will grow brown again, old fellow," my companion replied. "By summertime you may be back to normal."

Only then did I recall Holmes's smiling sociability toward Dudley at breakfast time. He had even given Dudley his allotment of sugar. I realized that the so-called sugar must have been a chemical concoction. It had bleached the colour out of Dudley's hair.

We put the luggage down and waited for a cab. Holmes was going to stay with his brother Mycroft.

"This is good-bye," I said shaking hands. My friend was on the point of responding when we were both diverted by the piercing sound of a police whistle.

Some distance away, a crowd had gathered beside a curio store. The centre of attention looked suspiciously like a body. We ran to the scene. I followed Holmes as he pressed to the centre of the crowd. In doing so I collided with someone bent on leaving. The collision produced a jingling sound like the one I had heard in the library, muffled now by the black cloak the person was wearing. Then the fellow dropped something. I retrieved it. It was a blowpipe, intricately carved in ivory. "Sir," I began, anxious to return it, but the owner had fled.

"Come on, Watson." Holmes had been made impatient by my encounter. He snatched the blowpipe from me. We were now at the centre of the crowd. On the icy pavement lay a body wrapped in heavy garments. To our horror we realized it was Waxflatter—and he had a knife in his chest!

"He went crazy," the storekeeper was explaining. "He just picked up a knife and stabbed himself."

Holmes stooped to the dying professor who, in a faint whisper, was trying to tell him something. One could barely discern the words. *"Eh-Tar,* Holmes," it sounded like. *"Eh-Tar."* Then his body went limp.

"Oh no!" Holmes pleaded, but there was nothing to be done. Rupert T. Waxflatter was dead.

Insensitive hands grabbed Holmes by the collar. "What in hell are you doing here?" said Lestrade.

In his distress Holmes tried to reason. "Mr. Lestrade," he said, "this has something to do with what we talked about. Please listen."

Lestrade turned to a constable. "Get these two schoolboys away from here," he ordered. The constable began forcibly to remove us. "Shove off," he said. "Go back to school. This ain't a sight for young eyes."

In the course of our long and honorable friendship I would see Holmes show profound grief on only two occasions. This was one of them.

Chapter Five

AFTER WAXFLATTER'S FUNERAL I WENT TO THE AT-
tic to see Elizabeth. It was a bitterly cold evening. The
windows revealed London as a frozen tableau. I found
her huddled before a dwindling fire in the dim glow of a
kerosene lamp, a blanket around her; she was a picture
of dejection. I felt inadequate to console her. The poor
girl was missing her guardian and, due to Holmes's
expulsion, the one person with whom she could truly
share her grief. Even Uncas the dog sensed his mistress's mood, for when I offered him a jam tart, which
I had obtained from the head boy's table, he took no
interest in it. I ate it myself to revive my own sagging
spirits.

I attempted conversation. Would she be staying on
in the professor's attic? She replied that the governors
had granted permission for her to remain there until
the end of the term, which was pretty short notice, I
thought. "After that I don't know where I will go," she
said pathetically. I knew she had no relations in America. In London the school, the dotty professor, and
Holmes had represented a family of sorts. I noticed

that she was holding fast to the professor's old cap, that low-crowned, close-fitting tweed object with its unusually broad peak. In the north of England I had seen hunters wear them when stalking deer. Elizabeth was clearly reluctant to let go of this souvenir of her departed guardian.

"I wish Holmes were here," she said in a voice tremulous with tears. "Uncle was very fond of him." I dabbed her eyes with my kerchief, but the effect was to provoke a new rush of tears. "You see, Watson," she said, "I simply do not believe that my uncle took his life."

"You must remember," I said in an effort to console her, "that the professor was a very old man. His mind could have snapped all of a sudden. That happens to old men."

This provoked a spirited defense of him. "My uncle's mind was sharper than the minds of men half his age. He was eccentric, I admit, but he wasn't unbalanced. No, Watson, he did not take his own life."

"Then what did happen?"

"He was murdered!" a familiar voice replied.

We turned and there was Holmes; he had entered through a skylight window with the agility of a lemur.

Elizabeth hugged him lovingly. Uncas rushed about in circles and now demanded the tart he had previously refused. Happily, I had another. Holmes still had Elizabeth in his arms.

"Lucky dog," I said, addressing Uncas.

When we settled, I decided that my best role in relation to Holmes was to play devil's advocate. "Come on now, Holmes," I said. "You heard the storekeeper's story. You saw the knife. Obviously, it was suicide."

"Never trust the obvious," he replied. "There are too many puzzling elements. Remember, there were two other so-called suicides. The professor knew about them. They were playing on his mind."

"Exactly," I said as if this proved my contention. But Holmes was now pacing up and down, concentrating. His method of investigation, he explained to me in later years, was to eliminate the impossible. Whatever remained, however improbable it seemed, was the key to the truth. What a formidable criminal he would have made!

Elizabeth said, "My uncle read newspapers every day. Sometimes he cut out items. He had certainly read of the deaths of Mr. Bobster and the Reverend Nesbit. And there was that visit to the attic by that strange old man. Do you remember?"

"That old man was at the funeral," said Holmes, revealing that he too had been present, for the governors had not invited him. But Holmes, determined to pay his last respects to his old mentor, had hidden in a tree. From this position he had caught sight of the other uninvited observer. He had given chase but had lost him in the thick shrubbery behind the church. He was quite sure it was the man who had come to the attic.

"In some way he is connected to all three murders," Holmes said, "and I am going to find him. If you agree, Elizabeth, I will make the attic my headquarters. My brother Mycroft is not in a position to offer me lodgings just now. In any case, I would much prefer to live here and work on the case. The school need not know. It will be a secret between us three. We are partners. Nobody will see me. Watson can bring in supplies and generally act as my assistant."

I thought that cavalier. If Holmes were caught, and it was a distinct possibility, I would be charged with complicity. This could lead to my expulsion, too, and the end of my hopes of a medical career. But Elizabeth was delighted with the idea.

"I can't jeopardize my own position," I said. It sounded pompous and Holmes looked at me with contempt. To console him, Elizabeth gave him the professor's deerstalker cap. It made him look much older, or perhaps memory is playing tricks with me. Perhaps, as I write, I am thinking of the Holmes of later years. Anyway, it certainly bucked him up.

Then Elizabeth turned her attention to me, fixing me for a moment with her beautiful blue-green eyes. I relented. "All right," I said. "I will do it." I was rewarded with a sisterly kiss.

Holmes returned at once to the subject at hand. "We have certain clues. For example, there were Waxflatter's dying words. Do you remember what he whispered? Two words—'Eh-Tar.' "

"A dying man's babbling," I said.

He paid no attention to this remark. Instead, he held up the blowpipe. "Do you recall anything about the man who dropped this, Watson?"

"Not much, except that he was in a hurry. A large fellow, bent on getting out of the crowd."

"Precisely. He was the only person anxious to leave the scene."

"He also jingled," I said. "Surely you did not miss that. Something on his body, something he was wearing, jingled. High-pitched. Very distinctive. I had heard it once before. I am sure I told you."

"Where?" Holmes was irritated. "Watson, where had you previously heard it?"

"In the library when I fell."

"Exactly where did you fall?"

"Onto the library floor, of course."

"No, I mean what *part* of the library? Was it in the sociology section, the history section? Where? It's important, Watson."

I replied that I would show him in the morning.

"You must," he said. "Tomorrow, after we have traced the owner of this blowpipe, we will visit the library again."

Our quest for the origins of the blowpipe took us next day to an unsalubrious part of St. Giles, where London was being torn apart in the construction of the great thoroughfares of Shaftesbury Avenue and the Charing Cross Road. Navvies had all but destroyed the original neighbourhood and only quaint pockets of it remained. One of them contained a shop owned by a certain Ethan Engel.

It was, incidentally, from this emporium of oddities and bric-a-brac that I bought the pipe for which Holmes would later become so famous. Indeed, I know it to be a fact that when Alfred Dunhill, the pipe specialist, opened his shop in the Strand some years later, he was asked on occasion, by American travellers, for a "Sherlock Holmes." In fact, Dunhill still gets such requests from customers, so closely did Holmes become identified with this type of pipe, its deep, full bend and enormous meerschaum bowl. You can see the original in surviving photographs of the great man.

But, of course, that was not the mission that took us to Engel that December day in 1870. Holmes hoped that the antiquarian would be able to throw some light on the blowpipe the mysterious stranger had dropped.

"It is Egyptian," said Engel, studying the artifact through thick-rimmed watchmaker's spectacles. "Egyptian craftsmanship. The ivory relief depicts Anubis, the Egyptian god of the dead."

I shuddered. Holmes was exhilarated. "Have you seen such a thing before?"

But the expert would not be hurried. "The work is exquisite. Very well preserved." With eyes bulbous behind the thick lenses, he was clearly covetous. "I have seen a blowpipe like this only once before. It was among a collection of Egyptiana I sold to a client. A tavern owner. Now, what was that name?"

Holmes could hardly contain himself. "Where can I find him?"

Engel consulted his book of transactions, thumbing through the pages, missing one and going back to it. He was in no mood to be rushed. "You are going to buy something, I assume." His eyes were on Holmes. It was a condition. If we bought something, Holmes would get the information.

"Buy something, Watson," Holmes urged me in a whisper. I said I was short of funds. "Come, Watson, this is not the time to be a pinchpenny. For goodness sake, make a purchase. This could lead us to the killer." And that was when I saw the pipe.

"Why on earth did you buy a pipe?" Holmes asked when we were in the street again. "It looks ridiculous."

It was certainly uncomfortable. It was so heavy that when the stem was between my lips I had to support the bowl in my hand. "It's distinguished," I said, "and I shall learn to smoke it." But to be perfectly honest, I hated the thing, though Holmes was clearly envious.

He wanted the pipe for himself. Such are the petty concerns of youth—I was determined that he shouldn't have it! But at least my purchase had secured for Holmes the information he needed. Engel had written down the name Khasek and an address in the East End of London.

We decided that our visit to the Lower Nile Tavern in Wapping would best be undertaken after dark. There were two principal reasons. First, as Holmes explained to me, such establishments catered to a late-night clientele. He didn't elaborate further and so I built up a picture in my mind of an eating house on the river where the well-to-do from more fashionable areas doubtless found it fun to dine. It probably offered an excellent North African cuisine, though personally I have no liking for spicy food. It would not be like that at all, Holmes advised me, but he remained as tight-lipped as ever.

The other reason for making the trip by night was the vital necessity to get Holmes off the school premises unobserved. We had decided that the only way of achieving this was to smuggle him in and out when the whole school was at assembly or in the dining hall. He seemed, by the way, insensitive to the fact that this would mean that I too missed dinner. Anyway, ever watchful for opportunities to fill my time, he suggested that in the interval between our return to school and our departure for Wapping I should obtain the supplies he needed to sustain him in the attic.

Now one might be excused for thinking that this would be a relatively simple matter, a dash to the corner tuck-shop for a banana and some buns. Not on your life. I was to become acquainted for the first time with Holmes's epicurean, not to say outlandish, tastes. How on earth, I asked him on being supplied with a list, was I to obtain pickled walnuts at that hour? And Lapsang souchong and Vichy water and sunflower seeds and roots of the mung bean? No doubt London was international enough to provide them. But surely it was unreasonable of him to expect me to shop for them, now! Elizabeth sympathized. He settled for bread, back bacon, and a pound of cheddar cheese.

But it was not just a matter of victualling Holmes. He demanded all manner of other items: litmus paper, chalk, invisible ink, a compass, and (for what reason, I was never to know) a supply of camphor balls! I was irritated beyond words. Moreover, he merely scoffed at my protest that these could only be obtained clandestinely from various school departments; he was asking me to steal. He merely muttered something about it all being in the cause of bringing villainy to book; he urged me to "soldier on," an expression I have never cared for, even after a career as an army medic.

Then there was the debate as to whether we should go to the tavern in disguise. I knew that he had developed much talent in the art of makeup and disguise, but frankly I didn't fancy walking the streets of London in some fancy attire. I put my foot down. We should go as ourselves, I said, because I was confident that whomsoever this Khasek fellow might be, he would more pleasantly receive two English schoolboys. Holmes reluctantly agreed, showing much tetchiness.

So at dusk we set off for Wapping. Rather than hire a hansom cab, the fare for which we suspected might be rather steep, we took the district railway. I recall that its western terminus at West Brompton had opened only that year. Of course, in those days the trains were hauled by squat tank locomotives (electrification came later that decade) and the steam from them further polluted the already unhealthy air. It was especially noxious that evening because a dense fog had come down. The engine plunged through yellow drifts of fog along a track between dun-coloured buildings on the way to Blackfriars. The line terminated there and Holmes proposed we should walk the rest of the way.

After we had crossed the new Blackfriars Bridge (it had been completed only the previous year), he spotted a bus going in our direction, and to my relief we boarded it. Already we were in a part of the city where I would not from choice have taken a stroll. Gas lamps left their moons in the encircling gloom and drunks staggered from noisy taverns. Sad-eyed children peered from the windows of murky tenements. On reaching Aldgate, however, the bus would take us no farther. The snow-packed road had become too treacherous; the driver feared for the horses. Thus we had no alternative but to disembark and stagger through the fog.

In the mean streets of the East End the only illumination was from candles flickering in back-to-back houses. The fog blinded us to whatever dangers lurked. Only an occasional ship's siren from the nearby river reassured us that a world beyond existed and was reachable. And it was into the labyrinthine alleys leading riverwards that Holmes looked for street names. At long last, more by luck than judgment, he found the one he was seeking: Saragosa Street.

At the foot of some steps was the Lower Nile Tavern. A heavy wooden door with an iron grille proclaimed its reluctance to admit strangers. Even Holmes, I think, was uneasy as he pulled a metal chain, which clanged a bell within. We could hear Eastern music, a shrill voice singing above the seductive pipings of ocarinas, and the pulse of tambourines. When the grille slid open, two suspicious eyes confronted us and widened with astonishment at the sight of two schoolboys at the door.

"Good evening," said Holmes pluckily. I managed an ingratiating smile.

"What do you want?" The voice was gruff and foreign. "Women?" I thought I saw Holmes wink as if in agreement, which did nothing to calm my nerves.

Holmes said, "We would like to talk to the owner." The grille shut, the door opened, and we were allowed inside. "Are you Khasek?" Holmes enquired. The doorman said nothing. He led us across a smokey salon to a dimly lit bar. At tables sat men of several nationalities and hybrids of as many more. They shot dice, played cards, and drank anise amid coarse tobacco fumes. From an improvised stage a belly dancer drew grins and catcalls. There were so many Arabs, Turks, and Armenians in that raucous assembly that we might have been in a casbah. I kept my hands in my pockets and hoped that Holmes's business would be brief.

"Can I get you boys a drink?" The offer came from a big fellow in a filthy turban; his unkempt beard stubble and unreliable eyes made him even less prepossessing.

"Do you have soup?" I ventured, then realized my mistake.

"Watson, please," said Holmes. I looked apologetically at our host.

With the knowledge I have now, I would recognize his racial origins as that of a Wazir or Affridi or other such Pathan tribe. Later in life I was to have many dealings with them on both sides of India's northwest frontier; they were a warlike people, very brave. But to my young and inexperienced eye on that occasion, he just looked frightening. Though he was amiable enough. "I am Khasek," he said.

Holmes came directly to the point. "Are you the owner of this establishment?" That sounded rather officious, even to me. It put Khasek on his guard. He nodded cautiously. Holmes took out the blowpipe and held it up. "Have you ever seen this before?"

What happened then was the last thing I could have expected. This burly, fearsome fellow blanched with fear! He took rapid steps backwards, staring at the blowpipe, and gave vent to an appalling scream. *"Rame Tep!"* he cried. *"Rame Tep!"*

Such was the commotion that the entire place fell silent. All eyes were on Holmes and me. Khasek regained some presence, but it was now a distinctly hostile one. Looking aghast at the blowpipe, he demanded to know whence it came. "I just happened upon it," replied Holmes, though he too was nervous now.

"Get out of here," roared the Pathan. "Go. Take it away."

"But, sir," said Holmes. "It is important that you give us any information you can about this object." Khasek glared at him. He called in their tongue to several Egyptians in the tavern. They sprang to their feet and came toward us with knives.

"Get out of my place," Khasek ordered, "or these words will be the last you hear."

Still, to my dismay, Holmes persisted. "Sir, would it be possible—" but Khasek now held a shotgun to his throat.

"We're leaving," said Holmes. "We're leaving right away." And we fled.

Outside we paused awhile. "He seemed quite determined to be rid of us, Holmes," I said, and we roared with laughter at my understatement. It was nearly midnight. The fog swirled in freezing circles. But compared with the atmosphere of the tavern, it seemed to us sublime. We began the slow trek back to West Brompton.

Chapter Six

I HAVE INTIMATED IN PAST WRITINGS, AS IN THE course of this, that there were times when I wearied of Sherlock Holmes. During the years at Baker Street, the great man's capacity to be impatient of the needs of others while in dedicated pursuit of a solution to a problem sometimes strained my deep regard for him. How much easier it was in those hot-blooded years of youth for differences of opinion about priorities suddenly to erupt. An example of this occurred on the night of our return from our adventure at the Lower Nile Tavern.

We had reached the school quadrangle, passing a night watchman slumbering peacefully beside a brazier at the lodge gate, when Holmes proposed that we should visit the library. I was both dismayed and indignant. It was already two in the morning. In less than five hours the bell would summon everyone to morning prayers—everyone except Holmes, who was not supposed to be on the school premises at all.

Surely, I said, the sensible thing was for him to go quietly to the attic where no doubt Elizabeth anxiously awaited him, while I retreated to my bed in the dormitory. I had already neglected my studies; if I failed to get at least some sleep I would be unable to catch up that day. Besides, to indulge in further nocturnal prowling was tempting fate; we were bound to be apprehended and I too would be expelled.

Holmes was insistent. He needed to be shown the precise place from which the jingling had come. It would indicate to him the reason the intruder had been in the library that day, which he believed to be connected with Khasek's alarmed cries of *"Rame Tep!"* and Waxflatter's last words, *"Eh Tar."* Well, I thought it all a bit far-fetched. I was also speechless with fatigue. Yet during the arduous walk from Wapping, it was Holmes who had complained. Now, apparently, he was quite recovered and as restless as a genie. He had no patience with my objections. So it was more from sheer exhaustion than from any confidence in the plan that I capitulated. In the stillness of the night we made our way to the library.

Any hope I might have fostered that it would be locked and prove impenetrable was dashed when Holmes, who invariably kept much gadgetry on his person, produced a skeleton key. Not surprisingly, he carried Swedish safety matches that enabled us to light a kerosene lamp that conveniently rested on the librarian's table. Thus equipped, we began to circumvent the shelves with the stealth of panthers.

Inevitably, Holmes showed impatience when I could not quickly locate the one from which I had fallen. Then I remembered Herodotus. If I could find the shelf containing the Greek historian, then the opposite side would be the position from which the jingling sound had come. Happily, under Classical Literature I found the spot. Holmes eagerly climbed steps on the other side, which to his satisfaction proved to be the *E–H* history section. His hands alighted on a work of Egyptology. I waited at the foot of the ladder for him to descend, but he indicated that I should raise the lantern high so he might make notes from the volume he was holding. "Please, Holmes," I implored, "write as fast as you can." Every minute seemed an hour in that situation, every creak from the building's ancient fabric, a threat of discovery. But Holmes was too enthralled to give my fears a second thought. "Incredible!" he blurted out.

"Holmes! Keep your voice down!"

"Yes, of course. I'm sorry, Watson." But this consideration was short-lived. "Oh, my God! Amazing!" he exclaimed, reacting to some further revelation, and the utterance echoed through the deserted room.

Standing there at the foot of the ladder like a Bartholdi lighthouse, I felt mounting resentment at the risks Holmes was taking. "Be quick, Holmes," I pleaded, fishing in my pocket for a pear drop. "Holmes, please." But the imperturbable researcher paid no heed. In fact, it would be a full hour before he felt sufficiently enriched by his discoveries to permit us to leave. And when at last I reached the dormitory pillow, sleep came insecurely. For in a comparatively short time, I would be roused by the bell.

All that day I went about my classes like a sleep-walker, consoled only by an awareness that I had already travelled the ground being covered. Due to the superiority of the teaching at my previous school, I was really not falling behind. On the contrary, my classmates were simply catching up. Nevertheless, at dinner I found myself with less than my usual appetite, a consequence of fatigue. I vowed I would not visit Waxflatter's attic that evening, a promise I did not keep.

I changed my mind for two main reasons. Demanding though he was, Holmes was my friend and intellectually far superior to the majority at Old Broms, whose students' limited interests and petty concerns I had begun to find unbearable. Holmes was never less than stimulating, and I had reason to believe he respected me. The usage he made at times of my good nature I could shrug off; he needed me as a sounding board for his theories, and I considered that a compliment. And, of course, there was Elizabeth, that rare girl whose capacity to enclose me in the aura of her love for Holmes was so endearing. Another reason for going to the attic that evening, I have to admit, was one of curiosity. I had to know where Holmes's investigations were leading. What was the significance of *Rame Tep?*

That evening Holmes gave me an account of his research, which he had continued to pursue with vigour in the attic all day. Elizabeth, it seemed, had located among her late uncle's possessions certain books which related to the subject, a development which Holmes regarded as more than merely coincidental. In later life, we were more than once to experience this phenomenon. It is as if books have a will of their own. If one's quest has integrity, books relevant to it have the ability to appear as if by magic. Or perhaps it is within man's power to draw knowledge to him in this way. I can only state that on occasions I have chanced upon (if chance is the operative word) a book, in a secondhand tray or staring at me from a library shelf, for which I had an urgent need yet least expected to find. Perhaps life is a road we have travelled. But, of course, this is not the place for speculation. Sufficient to say that strewn about the attic now were volumes on Egyptology.

Holmes was relaxed and Uncas slept at Elizabeth's feet. It was time to review the situation. Holmes reminded us that no civilization more than ancient Egypt's had based its religious and social life, in fact its entire culture, on the great central idea of immortality. Throughout existence, the chief concern of an educated Egyptian under the dynasties was of life beyond the grave. His procurement of a tomb and its furniture were priorities. It absorbed his mind and accounted for a sizeable share of his worldly wealth. Always he was mindful of the time when his mummified body would be borne to a house on a hill, a home more permanent than any he could hope to know in life. Of course, our knowledge of the doctrine of the resurrection and future life as held by ancient Egyptians is fragmentary. Their sages and scribes considered it unnecessary to document this for posterity because there already existed a holy work which said all that was necessary: the religious text known as the Book of the Dead.

Written on papyrus and deposited in the tomb of the deceased, these scriptures were timeless. They were based on the experience of more than five thousand years. They reflected the sublime beliefs and aspirations of Egyptian civilization. They also showed, in the form of amulets, charms, and magical rites, a reverence for superstitions. In the same way, Christianity would subsequently carry forward in its rituals some of so-called pagan origin.

Indeed, the central tenet of Christianity probably sprang from ancient Egypt's belief in resurrection. This had origins in nature, in the seasonal floodings of the Nile, which made the parched earth fertile and created life anew. At its pivot was the relationship of Rar, the sun god, to Osiris, the god of the dead, a parallel relationship to that between Christ and Almighty God. Indeed the chief drama of all religions is one of death and rebirth. That it began in the Egyptian delta was not surprising because the natural cycle of nature was very evident there.

Osiris, then, was the god of the resurrection as Christ became for Christians. Osiris was of divine origin, the son of Rar. He suffered death at the hands of evil, and after a struggle with these forces he rose again. It seemed logical, therefore, that those who believed in him would do likewise, providing the age-old burial customs were meticulously observed.

Egyptian dead were mummified in imitation of the mummified form of Osiris. The process of preservation developed into a science involving secret formulas. Methods constantly were being improved upon. A hierarchy evolved around the craft. At its summit was a deity. This was Anubis, the god of embalming.

Even after embracing Christianity, they continued to mummify their dead, mingling their worship of Christ with that of Osiris and the gods of antiquity. Yet the Christians, while preaching the doctrine of resurrection, insisted that there was no need to mummify. They taught that it was a useless custom. The chosen would receive their bodies back, intact, by the grace of God.

I must digress here. In later life, neither Holmes nor I would have described ourselves as practising Christians. I never knew him to attend mass. I think it is reasonable to say that his questioning mind and scientific approach to life annulled the teachings of what I believed to have been a Catholic upbringing. But I am equally certain that he was a man of great spirituality, more mystic than ecclesiastic. His outlook on such matters was eclectic. He selected from all the faiths what seemed pertinent to the search for ultimate truth. This extended, it may interest my reader to know, to psychic phenomena in later years. During at least one investigation he consulted a medium. As for myself, medical experience methodically reduced my capacity to respect the more rigid and least plausible tenets of established belief. However, Victorian England, like ancient Egypt, displayed ample evidence of the hope that the body would survive. One only had to look at the tombs of the wealthy in our graveyards. Their size and opulence surely suggested such aspirations. But to return to my narrative. . . .

The custom of making mummies gradually became obsolete and worship of Osiris diminished. But there was an exception to this mainstream evolution. Around 2500 B.C., when the Great Pyramid was young, there arose at Abydis, in southern Egypt, a sect that began to practise a distorted form of the central belief in survival. It was founded by a priest whose elders had rejected him, believing him to be corrupt and decadent. This, in fact, was true: his cult was a depraved convolution of the ancient faith. Its deity was Anubis, the jackal-headed god of embalming.

According to this cult, the living periodically had to be sacrificed if resurrection for all were to be assured. Young girls in their puberty were the preferred victims of this odious religion, in essence a fertility cult. These sacrificial victims were mummified alive. Although the authorities attempted to rid society of the sect, which had become widespread and universally feared, they merely succeeded in driving it underground. It became a secret society. The name of the founder was Rame Tep.

Holmes had discovered that Rame Tep were experts in the manufacture of drugs from various plants and their roots. For the innocents they intended to mummify, they used a drug which induced a trancelike state. Against their enemies they used a drug which brought about hallucinations. When it entered the bloodstream it produced nightmares so horrific and yet so real that the sufferer could not distinguish illusion from reality. It was a case of "whom the gods would destroy they first make insane."

Holmes then revealed a most remarkable fact. He had learned that Rame Tep used a thorn, no bigger than a pin, and a blowpipe as a method of injecting these foul potions into their victims. The darts were made from slivers of palmwood and impregnated with the drug. Tribes in the jungles of Ecuador still use blowpipes and darts to shoot prey in the tops of the giant ceiba trees. The victim hardly feels the missile enter the body and, of course, distance preserves the perpetrator's anonymity.

"But Holmes," I said, "an hallucination is not a

murder weapon, however unpleasant the effects. It is, after all, an abstract. Surely you can't kill someone with an hallucination."

"I think you can, Watson," he said. "I think you can cause death by such means. Think of what most repells you. It could be snakes, or spiders or bats or rats. These commonly are inducers of phobias. Others fear fire or water to an abnormal degree. These fears, as you know, are primordial. Well, Watson, suppose the effect of the dart was to induce in you a fear of unbearable magnitude. Suppose that fear became a living reality. It might cause you to act irrationally, even to the point of self-destruction. It might impel you to jump from a window or leap in front of a moving carriage in your desperation to get away from such insupportable horror. People can be literally scared to death, Watson."

"You mean you could even stab yourself in sheer panic, as poor Waxflatter may have done? But why, Holmes, would anyone wish harm to such a fine fellow? And how could you possibly connect it with Rame Tep, a religious sect that came into being five thousand years ago? After all, Holmes, we are living in the heart of civilization and this is the nineteenth century!"

Holmes's expression was one I would see many times over the years. It was an ironic, intimidating mask.

"Very good, Watson," he said. "You are becoming quite a detective. Your questions are first-rate. The reality, however, is that they cannot as yet be answered."

"But we can be certain of one thing," said Elizabeth.

"And what is that?"

"The murderer is within the precincts of the school."

"A rash statement, my dear, surely," Holmes said. "No doubt you are thinking of the sound Watson heard in the library."

"But I heard it too, in the courtyard," she said. "Uncas chased that figure in the dark. He was chasing a jingling sound."

Holmes seemed caught off guard. "Of course."

"And he bit off a scrap of a black cloak. I tried to take it from him. It's possible he brought it back here."

"Good God!" Holmes exclaimed. "What are we waiting for? We must search every inch of the attic. We must find that swatch of material."

I don't know whether I am unique in this, I rather suspect that I am not, but one of my least favorite occupations is hunting for something lost. You see, I have always credited inanimate objects with wills of their own; they actually hide. I have only to drop a button or an egg spoon from the breakfast table, and in the short period of time it takes to reach the floor, it will decide to travel, adopt a measure of camouflage, and only when it is ready, will it reveal itself. How unlikely it was then, I reflected, that we would come upon that piece of cloth amid the clutter of the professor's belongings. Besides, we had no certainty that it was there. But whatever gods hold sway over these lesser forms of life, they were with us on that evening. Within an hour, during which I discovered four left-handed shoes ("There is only one shoe, Watson," Holmes explained, "it's simply that Uncas is bringing the same shoe back to you"), Elizabeth was heard to exclaim, "I've found it!" Inside the old man's toolbox, it adhered to a tack.

Holmes, of course, was thrilled. This was the first piece of tangible evidence. He began at once to subject it to scientific scrutiny. This meant that I was again required to raid the stores for chemicals. He had also become even more persnickety about his dietary needs. I scoured a local street market for a particular crustacean I knew to be available only when the equinoctial tides off Normandy washed it ashore. Holmes considered it to be brain fodder. (I am glad to say that he settled for potted shrimps.) Soon he was able to announce progress: The cloth had at some time been treated with an industrial spirit, no doubt as a method of removing a stain. This spirit he identified as the product of a firm called Frogit and Frogit, with warehouses at Shad Thames, south of the river. He proposed that the three of us should visit there.

I expected the warehouse to be as busy as a hive. The docklands are the arteries of our great Empire of which London is the heart. Activity never ceases there. But we found instead a lofty building from which prosperity had flown. Rats had taken over this ruin in a cul-de-sac. Barrels that bore the firm's name had shed their contents; machinery had rusted; here and there a door flapped in the chilly wind. We had to gain entry through a window jagged with broken glass. Then we gingerly trod floorboards that threatened to give way. A rat scuffled in the debris. Holmes then glimpsed something in the darkness. Protruding from the rotting floor was a pyramid-shaped structure some four feet high. On closer examination we found it to be made of stone. More intriguing still were its embellishments: Egyptian hieroglyphics and ancient artwork depicting a primeval rite.

"It's a statue," I said.

"No, Watson, it is not."

"Then what is it?"

Elizabeth and I waited for an explanation while Holmes walked around the structure. "It is merely the tip of an iceberg," he said enigmatically.

I was on the point of probing him further when there was an earsplitting sound of breaking timber. The floor below us gave way. Holmes, Elizabeth, and I were plunged forward. We careened down a slope to the level below. Dusting off splinters and bits of masonry, we realized that we were now at the base of a much larger pyramid of which we had hitherto seen only the tip. It was some fifty feet high. We walked around its walls, In one, a staircase had been constructed; it spiralled down to an even lower level. In another was a trap door. We entered this and came to a tunnel wide enough only for us to crawl through. Visible at the other end were holes through which light shone.

"Let's get out of here," I said, but there was no stopping Holmes now. Like moles in a burrow we moved toward the light. What we saw through the holes might have passed for some bizarre theatrical fantasy. But it was not. It was diabolically real.

Chapter Seven

THE THAMESIDE PARISHES OF SHADWELL, WAPPING, and Limehouse are flanked on their shoreline by warehouses which, from the river, look as forbidding as a prison wall. In the times I am writing about, some ten thousand ships every year discharged into them the raw materials and merchandise that fed the world's greatest city. Behind this panoply of commerce, disparate communities flourished, each with customs and traditions and pleasures imported from distant homelands.

The Chinese had established their quarter in Limehouse, along the East India Dock Road; the Irish were in Spitalfields and Shadwell; the Jewish communities were in Aldgate and Stepney; the Lascars, who were Indian crews of British ships, were everywhere as were immigrants from Arabia, Africa, Mozambique, and the islands of the South Pacific.

There were mosques and temples and synagogues. There were opium dens. In the brothels, many of the prostitutes were French and Italian. Some parts of the

East End were so dangerous that the police declined to patrol them; to many corruptions they turned a blind eye. Much of what was arcane and secretive and sinister in Victorian life thrived in dockland, conveniently distanced behind the screen of respectability through which society chose to view itself. And it was the perfect setting in which to hide from scrutiny the unspeakable rite we were about to witness, and for which this derelict warehouse provided a perfect camouflage.

We were looking through the hollow eye of a religious idol which seemed to be animal in form, with two truncated arms spreading below us in a gesture of embrace. Judging by the size of these protuberances, which had a shell-like texture like a monstrous crustacean, the god itself was enormous. It was clearly the centrepiece of an elaborate altar, flanked on each side by other gods, some with human faces and lionesque trunks, others wholly human in form, with smooth bodies and the features of youth preserved for eternity in stone. There were sarcophaguses, crudely riven with hieroglyphics, beautiful tapestries, papyruses stretched on wooden frames, all of which proclaimed the ancient Egyptian nature of this gawdy temple, while flaming chandeliers, suspended from the vaulted ceiling, gave it an embrace of devout mystery, which belied the depravity of the ceremony in progress there.

Wearing a hood in the likeness of a jackal's head and a cloth-of-gold robe, a high priest was incanting in an alien vernacular before some fifty supplicants. They wore terracotta-coloured gowns and their heads were shaven, except for a strand of hair cut and dyed green to resemble a serpent. At their wrists were suspended carved ivory blowpipes, similar to the one which had come into our possession, and little leather pouches we were sure must contain the thorns they shot from them.

At the bidding of the high priest, the idolators raised their arms in homage to the altar god; this produced a crescendo of the jingling sound with which we were familiar. It was caused by the movement of the gem-studded amulets they wore.

Beside the altar, a strapping fellow of Nubian appearance was attending a green urn in which some unguent substance bubbled vaporously, while in front of it the body of a pubescent girl was being shrouded with the liniments of burial. To our horror we realized that the young innocent was alive, although apparently in a trance, and we stared in disbelief as she was led, like a sleepwalker, to an open coffin and lifted into it.

Holmes broke the spell into which this outrage had thrust us. "These fiends are followers of the Rame Tep cult," he said. "I am going down to the temple."

He returned through the tunnel and reappeared below us, hidden from the assembly by an ornamental pillar. The chanting by now had reached an hysterical pitch. All eyes were on the coffin. I saw Holmes steal up behind one man and deftly remove a pouch of thorns from his belt, intending, no doubt, to subject them to analysis when we were safely back in the attic, though the prospect of so agreeable an outcome grew more remote as I faced the facts of our predicament. Holmes was sure to be spotted and then we would all be in dire trouble. We had intruded upon a secret society. They would certainly not spare our lives.

The dreadful rite had reached its climax. Fluid from

the vat was being transferred to the coffin. The hapless victim was being mummified—alive!

"Stop, you murderers!" Holmes shouted, and my heart missed a beat. The chanting stopped. All eyes turned in his direction, and in a sudden rush the cultists moved toward him, blowpipes raised with a view to kill. Holmes ran for his life.

We caught up with him at the spiral stairway. Once we had climbed it, we hurled down upon our pursuers as many empty barrels as we could lay our hands on, and this delayed their progress. While doing so we were caught in a rain of their poisonous thorns, which pricked at our flesh like gnat bites. But we were too intent upon escape to ponder the inevitable consequence.

We bolted across the creaking floor to the broken window beyond which was the cul-de-sac. This would lead us back to the city streets and relative safety. Once in the open we believed we had shaken them off, but then a particularly vicious member of the cult, armed with a murderous blade, leapt out of the window we had clambered through. We panicked. We fled in the wrong direction and came to a dead end. The cul-de-sac was blocked by a high railing which, nevertheless, we scaled, only to find ourselves in a graveyard where the light of the moon on the impacted snow made gaunt shadows of the funereal statuary and morbid tombs. We were in a country of the dead.

Due to our exertions, the drug in our systems was beginning to take effect. At first it produced a pleasant sense of well-being. We became complacent. Our foes might be close at hand, but we no longer gave them a thought. The forlorn monuments about us lost their ability to intimidate. Indeed, we wanted to laugh at their gross ostentation. We giggled as we walked. Holmes put an arm around Elizabeth, she snuggled up close, and I followed them in a spirit as carefree as would have befitted a country ramble. But this was short-lived. Euphoria turned to a vague sense of dread. We were about to experience the terrors of hallucination.

Elizabeth was the first to lose grip of reality, although I must have been approaching a similar condition myself, for I distinctly saw the skeleton of an arm protrude from a grave and grab her leg. I saw her reel back in horror. Yet I was still sufficiently in command of my senses to ask Holmes what was happening.

"Elizabeth is beginning to hallucinate," he said with a worried yet controlled expression. "We shall have to tie her down." He spoke calmly to the frantic girl. "It isn't real, Elizabeth. You are just imagining it all." But by now the girl was screaming.

"Come, Watson, give me your braces." Of course, in the circumstances I did not hesitate. I handed him my scarf as well. We were about to secure her to a gravestone when she stepped backwards and fell into an open grave. "Uncle, please!" She was calling out in terror. "No, Uncle, please!" Her disturbed mind, I would learn later, was creating the illusion that her late guardian was burying her alive, standing over the grave and shovelling earth upon her. Of course, these details of her delirium were unknown to me then. In any case, I too was experiencing fantasies of my own which rendered me helpless to assist Holmes in whatever precautions he was attempting to take to save us from injuring ourselves.

The reader is entitled to ask what form my hallucinations were taking, even though across the years a certain sense of shame still overtakes me when I recall them. But I have always shared with Holmes a reverence for putting facts on record, which denies me the constraint of reticence. You see, in my drug-abused mind, I was being attacked by figments of food! All manner of comestibles which I had taken so much pleasure in consuming were now intent upon eating me! Pies, sweetmeats, and puddings had developed spindly limbs and were swarming all over my body, pinning me down until I was a helpless Gulliver in some outlandish Lilliput.

Of one thing I am sure, neither Elizabeth nor I would have lived to tell the tale had not Holmes through some superior element in his metabolism been able to ward off his own fall into the quagmire of fantasy until such time as he had taken measures to prevent us from inflicting harm upon ourselves. By what must have been a superhuman effort of will he managed to tie us both to gravestones, using our scarves and my braces before succumbing, himself, to the strange deceits and whimsicalities which that night were to eat into his brain like worms. For, judging by the account he gave me later, or, to be more exact, from his reluctance to discuss the matter in detail, I was to conclude that his ordeal had been the most agonizing of all.

As it transpired, after securing us, Holmes had decided to wait for sunrise. Nearby an unused vault appeared to offer shelter, but as he entered its crypt-like interior, it suddenly changed into the parlour of his childhood home. His hallucinations had begun.

The scene was not a happy one. In those surroundings so familiar to him, his parents were engaged in a bitter argument. He tried to comfort them only to be accused by his father of being the cause of the quarrel. "You have destroyed my life. Now I will destroy yours," were the terrible words his father spoke. This heartbreaking vision changed again. Now the figure of his father was transformed into that of a Rame Tep fanatic, brandishing a knife with which he proceeded to lunge at the distraught youth. Holmes could not distinguish fact from fantasy. All he knew was that in the nightmare world, someone was coming toward him, knife in hand. He was going to die. Then a shot rang out.

Holmes found himself looking into the barrel of a gun. Reality had returned. He saw the silhouette of a Rame Tep follower scuffling away in the distance, limping as if from a wound. The gun aimed at Holmes was being held by a powerful fellow who evidently had been roused from his bed, for he had thrown a coat over his nightshirt. This was the church caretaker and he had been disturbed by the commotion. He helped Holmes untie us and then announced his intention of taking us to the nearest police station where we would be charged with trespass.

Secretly, I was relieved by this outcome. For in my opinion the irate church official had saved our skins. But Holmes gave that aspect of the situation scant consideration. In no time at all he was his indignant self again, complaining bitterly that the charge was false and demanding that Detective Sergeant Lestrade of Scotland Yard be informed of our predicament. More, he wanted Lestrade brought to the constabulary. Holmes's ploy worked; the local police were sufficiently intimidated, by the mention of Scotland

Yard, to send an urgent message to Lestrade. In due course the harassed detective arrived, purple with anger.

He raged at Holmes. "This is the very last occasion on which you will waste my time," he said. "Why can't you behave like ordinary kids! Do you want to end up in the jug? This is your last chance. I've talked to the church authorities and they will drop the charge, but if ever . . ."

"But Mr. Lestrade," Holmes urged, "I beg of you to investigate. This fanatical cult is feared throughout the city. The Muslim community is particularly frightened. Young girls are being abducted for use in disgusting rituals. I am convinced there is a connection too with the deaths of Bobster, Nesbit, and Professor Waxflatter. There may have been other mysterious deaths. You must investigate."

"Investigate what?" Lestrade was at the end of his tether. "All this is the product of your fertile imagination. Damn it, Holmes, I don't have to justify myself to you. This is pure nonsense. I have been in the force for seven years and you presume to know more about the underworld than I do. What arrogance! Now, leave, all three of you. Simply leave!"

Holmes turned once more to Lestrade. "Very well. But I suggest you ask your laboratory people to analyse these." From the leather pouch he tipped a few of the thorns into Lestrade's hand. "You may be in for a surprise."

"Just get out!"

As we were leaving I had time to notice that one of the thorns had stuck to the detective's palm. He plucked it out and contemptuously discarded it.

Chapter Eight

DURING MY LONG AND INTIMATE ACQUAINTANCE with Sherlock Holmes I was never to hear him refer to his family relationships and hardly ever to his early childhood. Those among my readers who have followed our adventures over the years will doubtless recall that in the *Memoirs* (more precisely in the account of the case of "The Greek Interpreter," which appeared in that volume), I considered this reticence on his part of sufficient importance to mention it. I believed it would help the public at large to better understand his character and the somewhat inhuman effect he was capable of producing upon me and upon others. It was as though he had sprung from some amorphous past, with a fully fledged intellect, a brain without a heart, a being as deficient in human sympathy as he was preeminent in intelligence; an isolated phenomenon.

In retrospect I feel that those remarks of mine in the *Memoirs* may have done him an injustice, for superhuman though at times he might have appeared, there was a compassionate side to him which by its very nature could not be generally known.

As I wrote in "The Adventure of Black Peter" (a case recounted in *The Return of Sherlock Holmes*), like all great artists, Holmes lived for his art's sake (although his art was more a science, the refined science of deduction) and the financial rewards of that art were of secondary consideration.

During the many years of our partnership I seldom knew him claim any large reward for his inestimable services. So unworldy was he—and so capricious—that he frequently refused his help to the powerful and wealthy, if the problem had no appeal to his sympathies, while he devoted weeks of intense application to the affairs of some humble client whose case presented those strange and dramatic qualities which appealed to his imagination and challenged his ingenuity. In other words, if poverty and injustice went hand in hand, as so often in urban life they tend to do, then Holmes was prepared to play Robin Hood, should the need arise, and be ready to absorb the costs of such endeavours.

Notwithstanding this aspect of his personality, Holmes in adult life was an essentially unemotional character, disinclined to form new friendships and so secretive of facts concerning his own people and his origins that I had come to believe he was an orphan with no living relations. But one day, to my very great surprise, he began to talk to me about his brother.

We were cosily relaxed one winter's night in Baker Street and had been discussing the subject of talent and how far any singular gift possessed by an individual was due to his ancestry, how far to early training. In his own case, I suggested, his peculiar facility for deduction and his faculties of observation were surely due to systematic training.

He answered thoughtfully. To some extent I was right, he conceded. His ancestors had been country squires who led lives natural to their class so he could not suppose that any particular gift he might possess had been inherited from them. Nevertheless, he admitted, there might be an hereditary link to powers of observation possessed by his grandmother. She had been the sister of Vernet, the French painter. But, he added wryly, art in the blood was liable to take the strangest forms.

Sensing on that evening that I could not agree that this was sufficient proof of an hereditary basis for his powers, he added that his brother, Mycroft Holmes, possessed them in larger degrees. "He is seven years my senior," he told me, "and he is my superior in observation and deduction."

This also I could not credit. Was it possible there were two such phenomena alive and living in London? In our school days I had known of Mycroft's existence. Indeed, Holmes had been intending to stay with him after his expulsion from Old Broms, changing his mind, I have no doubt, only when the idea of sharing the attic with Elizabeth seemed so much more appealing. But on this much later occasion when Holmes spoke of his brother, I could give no credence to the notion that there was another genius of detection other than the one whose cases I had been chronicling.

I said he was simply being overly modest in crediting his brother with talents superior to those I admired in him. And if there really were two Holmeses, how was it that one had managed to remain unknown?

Holmes was insistent. Mycroft was the true master, but he added that his brother did not use his powers for detective work; he was too idle. If he did, if the art of the detective began and ended in reasoning from an armchair, Holmes added, then his brother would be the greatest criminal agent that ever lived. Curiously, that was the description I would ultimately apply to my friend Sherlock Holmes.

At any rate, there came a time when I was introduced to Mycroft Holmes, an occasion I have described in the *Memoirs*. Holmes took me to meet him at the Diogenes Club, a curious institution with rooms near the Carlton just off Pall Mall. He was a much larger and stouter man than Holmes, extremely corpulent, but his face, though massive, had preserved something of the sharpness of expression which was so remarkable in that of his brother. His eyes, which were of a peculiarly light, watery grey, seemed always to retain that faraway, introspective look which I had only observed in Sherlock's when he was exerting his full powers of concentration. I instinctively liked him and I am quite proud to say that during that meeting Mycroft made a remark which I deemed to be highly complimentary, notwithstanding the pained look I perceived on Sherlock's face when his brother spoke it. "I hear of Sherlock everywhere since you became his chronicler," he said.

Well, my excuse for reminiscing in this self-indulgent way about an event beyond the canvas of my narrative (one that was much in the future, in relation to the story I am telling) is that when we next met in the attic after that night in the graveyard, Holmes's reluctance to describe the nature of his hallucinations was an early indication of his reticence in all matters related to his childhood. Only later would he hint at the content of his nightmare, and the significance of that painful vision of an unhappy family sanctum. In the attic he showed what I considered to be an unconscionable sympathy with and interest in the details of Elizabeth's ordeal and merely shook with laughter at mine.

In pursuit of his desire to connect the death of Waxflatter and the others with the activities of Rame Tep, Holmes had set me a most trying task. At his behest I was sifting through the late professor's papers, several files of them which, I need hardly mention, were in a frightful muddle. That he had not compartmentalized his interests was clear from those bulging folders. Scientific charts, drawings, mathematical formulae, and lecture notes were all mixed up with his personal correspondence. Even shopping lists had been stuffed into these overflowing wallets which proclaimed the character of the man, evidence of immense industry and very little method.

I was amused to discover that the old man had acquired the habit of writing little notes to himself. These random examples reflect, I think, his will-o'-the-wisp nature—"Must write Haslam-Hopwood about Stark's Theory of Levitation," "Buy pork pie at Frampton's," and "Bronya's cat run over—send condolences," "Odd sock, blue with yellow spots, in my laundry. Is it Snelgrove's?" and "Chronic fault in machine's hydraulics," "Order pot of bloater paste."

There were diaries galore, the earliest dating back to the early eighteen hundreds; postcards from foreign lands, sent by former pupils on the Grand Tour; concert programmes and, intriguingly, since I knew he had been a lifelong bachelor, several illustrated catalogues of women's corsetry, amply illustrated. What an odd old cove he had been, I thought. I came upon a small, unframed canvas, which had been folded several times, causing cracks and crease marks over what I assumed to be a painting of a group of sixth-form Brompton scholars on their graduation day. Holmes would surely be interested in that, I decided, if simply for historic reasons, because it showed how student fashions had changed since 1812, the date with which it was inscribed. Indeed, one of the young men the artist had depicted in graduation attire might even be Waxflatter himself, I mused. So I showed it to Holmes.

"Quite a painting, eh, Holmes?" I said good naturedly.

"Clues, Watson!" he said, pushing it away impatiently. "I want clues, not art critiques!" Really, Holmes could be damnably bad-mannered.

And it was not as if he were contributing to the search, himself. He wanted clues, but what was he doing to find them? He was occupied in what I could only describe as tinkering, hammering lightly but with nerve-jangling persistence on a bit of the old man's flying machine; it looked like a strut of a wing.

"Holmes," I said. "Could you please stop that infernal hammering? It is aggravating my headache which, by the way, I have had ever since those awful hallucinations."

"It helps me to think."

"I can't think at all," I said. "I have lost too much sleep."

"No time for sleep," he said. "We must continue

working. We have got to find a clue. Something that links Waxflatter with Rame Tep!''

Holmes was at his most infuriating. I could have hurled the painting at him there and then. I returned to the files, stuffed the painting back into its folder, and glared at him. He was not aware of my hostility and went on tap, tap, tapping on the metal strut. I could more easily have borne his violin. On the sofa Elizabeth dozed contentedly, Uncas snugly beside her, neither troubled by Holmes's tinkering. They probably found it soporific. If only I could do likewise. I was tired and bored and intimidated by the task Holmes had set me, compromised by his expectations.

It was no use; I simply could not look through any more files. Evidence of a lifetime of muddle was already heaped around me. To blazes with clues! Holmes could look for them himself. I was just too sleepy.

Then I noticed on a nearby table a plate on which sat a French pastry and a fork. It was certainly appetizing, but I recalled that an identical confection had been among the many which had attacked me during my hallucinations. Would this one sprout legs and do the same? Gently, I lifted the fork to it. Was it real or an illusion? Would it speak if spoken to? "Now, Mr. Pastry," I whispered, "have you anything to say? Are you what you seem or a figment of a dream?" No answer. Surely it was good enough to eat. I touched it.

"Watson!"

Good heavens, had it spoken? No, I had dozed off; Holmes was shaking me. "Watson, wake up!" His excitement was intense. "Watson, what have you done with that painting?" I fished it out of the file and gave it to him.

"My god, Watson, do you realize what you have stumbled on?"

"A painting of Waxflatter's graduation?"

"Exactly. And who is standing beside the professor?"

I waited for him to tell me.

"Bobster."

"Bentley Bobster?"

"The very same. The accountant who, according to *The Times* of December twelfth, took his life in Pimlico." He turned the canvas over. "Look, Watson, the names are written on the back—Rupert T. Waxflatter, Duncan Nesbit, Oscar Hallmark—names I remember from newspaper obituaries. They all died recently in unusual ways. Good show, Watson. I am proud of you."

But I had no time to react to Holmes's praise, because at that moment the door of the attic was thrust open. It was Rathe. "Holmes," said our unexpected caller, "I did not expect our foils to cross so soon." Holmes's dismay was profound. It was Rathe's manner, not merely the fact that he had discovered us, that startled him. He seemed to expect some sympathy from the master he most admired, but clearly it was not forthcoming.

"What is the meaning of this, Holmes?" Rathe continued. "What are you doing here? You were forbidden to enter school precincts. Come to my study, the three of you."

I do not know what instinct prompted me, but on seeing Rathe's expression, which registered not only anger but fear, I hid the graduation picture under my shirt. Something told me that it was for our eyes only.

"Well, Holmes, what have you been poking your

inquisitive nose into?" Rathe was now seated in his study. Still perplexed by Rathe's manner, Holmes countered with a question of his own.

"How did you know I was hiding in Waxflatter's attic?"

"Have you forgotten that we share the same powers of deduction?" Rathe replied tartly.

Holmes looked sceptical. There was a knock on the door and Mrs. Dribb entered. Our presence, particularly that of Holmes, surprised her.

"You wanted me, Mr. Rathe?"

"I need your assistance with these students, Mrs. Dribb."

"But I thought young Mr. Holmes had left the school."

"We were all under that impression," said Rathe. "Unfortunately, Mr. Holmes has landed himself in an even more serious mess." His voice became sterner. "If the board of governors were to know of this transgression, Holmes, they could well have you arrested. Do you fancy being sent to prison?"

Holmes could hardly believe his ears. What had happened to the gallant fencing master who had championed his cause, defended him against the injustice for which he had been expelled?

Rathe relented slightly. "But there is no need to tell the board." A thoughtful pause. "Holmes, I am willing to forget about this, providing that tomorrow you leave as originally planned." Then he turned to me. "You will do the same, Watson."

It came as a body blow. "Sir, you mean—"

"I mean that if I were to take this matter before the board you too would be summarily expelled. I am merely saving you from that disgrace."

What I had feared all along had come to pass. I felt crushed. My association with Holmes had put an end to my school days, my hope for a university place, a medical career. Self-pity welled up inside of me, rendering me speechless. Rathe was now talking to Elizabeth.

"I find your behavior inexcusable too, young lady," he was saying. "Was it with your permission that Mr. Holmes stayed in your uncle's laboratory?"

She nodded.

"I find that extraordinarily immodest in a girl of sixteen."

Elizabeth flushed. Mrs. Dribb gave her a look of disgust. Turning to Rathe, the matron said malevolently, "May I suggest, sir, that we have the dog taken to the pound? I know of no other school which permits pets on its premises."

"No, no," cried Elizabeth. "You can't do such a cruel thing."

"I agree, Mrs. Dribb. And I want Waxflatter's laboratory cleared. Dispose of everything. We need the space for legitimate school activities."

Holmes turned on him angrily, "But, sir, the attic is full of the professor's research. His inventions are there. There are papers of scientific value. All manner of vital documents. It holds the key to his whole life's work."

"His life is over," Rathe said raspingly.

"You have no right," said Holmes, beyond himself.

"No right, Mr. Holmes? Your tone surprises me. Especially when you use it to me."

The reprimand revived Holmes's confusion, having appealed to their former loyalty. "I'm sorry," he said. "I got carried away."

Rathe sat back and studied us. After a while he spoke again. "You will have to stay here overnight. At so late an hour we would find it difficult to get you transportation." To Mrs. Dribb he said: "Take the two boys to Room Fourteen-B. They can spend the rest of the night there. The young lady must be in a separate room. I suggest the one next door to your own."

We followed the matron from the study, but Rathe called Holmes back. "Remember what I tried to teach you, Holmes," he said. "Control your emotions or they will control you. Emotion could be your downfall."

"Yes, sir," said Holmes meekly, and then he joined us in the corridor.

Uncas was put in a broom closet. Elizabeth was taken to a nearby room. We entered Room 14B and heard Mrs. Dribb turn the key in each door. We had been locked up for the night. From the empty hallway came the sound of little Uncas, whining pitifully.

Room 14B was like a prison cell. Many a poor wretch had been detained there before us, I was sure. There was no illumination, save that reflected through a high fanlight window from the snow outside. We could make out a soiled mattress on a dingy bed and peeling paint on bare walls. What a place to spend my final hours at Brompton! I paced up and down like a primate in a zoo and fumed at Holmes. "I knew we would be caught. I knew it, Holmes. All this may be an amusing escapade for you, but it has cost me everything. I wish I had never become involved with you. Holmes! You might at least listen. What are you doing?"

He had stripped the bed of the mattress and had propped the frame against the farthest wall. Using it as a ladder, he had reached the fanlight, which he had unlatched, and was now peering down at whatever lay below. He reappeared and called to me. "We can leave now," he said. "Come and have a look."

Less nimble than Holmes, I made heavy work of joining him at the top of the bedframe. I looked through the fanlight and perceived that we were some five storeys from the ground. At least a hundred feet below, the courtyard sparkled in the hard frost. The scene induced a short spasm of vertigo.

"You're mad," I said. "I'm staying put."

He looked downcast. "You disappoint me, Watson. We are on the verge of cracking this case."

"If we go out of that window the only thing we'll crack is our skulls," I said. "There isn't even a ledge."

"But there is a gutter," he said, indicating the rusting rain trough under the eaves, which looked incapable of supporting a cat. "I can hold on to that and make my way to the next window." He began to plead. "I need you, Watson. Don't desert me now. We are in this together. We are a team."

"A losing team," I said dejectedly. But I knew I would not deflect him from what he had made up his mind to do. Over the years I would come to know that Holmes's life was a testimony to the unconquerable power of the human will. Nevertheless, at this moment I was convinced that he would kill himself.

He clambered up and grabbed the gutter, swung himself through the fanlight, and began to move along the side of the building, clutching the fragile rain trough, which creaked ominously. From my vantage point I could see what he could not: a section of the guttering had rusted away, leaving a gap where Holmes might well place a hand, with fatal consequences. I could also see a means by which I could reach the roof and thereby attempt to save him.

If I leaned backwards out of the fanlight, I conjectured, I might actually somersault onto a part of the roof directly above me, which would provide me with a standing position, since it seemed flat to the touch. I closed my eyes and did so. I landed at the very moment when the gutter broke beneath Holmes's weight. Now he was dangling head downwards, at the extremity of a strip of metal attached to the main gutter by a slender, rusting thread. I grabbed his trouser leg. Now, quite literally, I had his life in my hands.

I cannot explain what perverse fancy brought the matter to mind just then, but I heard myself say, "Holmes, I have solved the riddle."

"Good for you, Watson," was his response from midair.

"The bear is white," I said.

"What is your reasoning?" enquired my aerobatic friend.

"Well," I said lamely. "It was a colour I had not already thought of."

"Solutions without evidence are quite useless," he called, "and if you don't haul me up soon, I will be useless, too."

He was right. The seam of one trouser leg was tearing. I gave the other an almighty tug, surprising myself at the strength I could muster, and brought him feet-first to safety. "Sorry about that," I said.

"Not at all, my dear Watson. I appear to be no worse for wear. But you really must reason more scientifically."

In the cold air, I was sweating. "I will, Holmes," I said. "I will."

We edged our way along the rooftop and came to a skylight through which, by the glow of a paraffin lamp, we could see Elizabeth reclining. She was quickly alerted when we tapped on the pane. She opened the window and we climbed inside. She cautioned us to be quiet, indicating a light beneath the door to the adjoining room: Mrs. Dribb.

Holmes whispered, "Have you still got the painting, Watson?"

I withdrew it from my shirt. He huddled around the lamp to examine it in detail. Holmes pointed to those who had recently died: Bobster, Nesbit, Waxflatter, Hallmark . . .

"Hallmark?" I enquired.

"Oscar Hallmark was the first of the group to die," Holmes explained. "The police found him in the Thames, a former member of Parliament."

"A conservative?"

"Really, Watson. Is that relevant? As a matter of fact he was a radical."

"Who is the fifth man?" I asked; there were five in the picture.

"Think, Watson. Isn't the face familiar? Remember, they were all in their teens when this was painted, in the year eighteen-twenty, according to the date on the back."

"And so they would be all in their seventies now."

"Very bright, Watson. Who have we encountered in the course of our investigations, other than those who have died, to fit that description?"

"Snelgrove?"

"Rubbish. Snelgrove was never young." Holmes was understandably bitter toward the master who had pressed for his expulsion. "Try again."

Then Elizabeth said brightly, "It's the man who visited my uncle. The man who ran away from the funeral."

He hugged her fondly. "Exactly, my love. His name is Chester Cragwitch. And doesn't it surprise you that he is still alive, the only surviving member of this group? We have got to find him."

"Fantastic work, Holmes," I said.

"Elementary, my dear Watson," he replied, and Elizabeth and I exchanged a knowing smile.

"Now this is what we must do. . . ." We listened carefully to his plan. Elizabeth would return to the attic, rescuing Uncas on the way. Holmes produced a skeleton key to the broom closet. In the attic Elizabeth would collect all the items of the professor's, to be saved before Mrs. Dribb could destroy them. A daunting task, I thought, but Elizabeth did not shrink from it. Meanwhile, Holmes and I would set off in search of Cragwitch, whom we had to reach before Rame Tep got to him.

Before we parted, Holmes took Elizabeth aside. They kissed so passionately that I did not know where to look. I tried the door. "It is locked," I said.

"So it is," said Holmes, momentarily interrupting his lovemaking. "Try this key. If it doesn't fit, we'll use the fanlight." Which is what we did.

When Elizabeth had left on her mission and we were crossing the school grounds, I asked Holmes where we were bound. "To Oxford," he replied. "Cragwitch lives in a country manor near there."

"But that is miles away. How are we to get there?"

"An omnibus will take us to Paddington. From there we'll catch the train. We should be there before sunset. We've plenty of time, Watson. No school today because it's Sunday, and next week is the end of term."

No school ever again, I reflected miserably, for now there was no way that I could avoid expulsion.

Chapter Nine

THE TRAIN WE CAUGHT AT PADDINGTON TURNED OUT
to be a meanderer of the first order, stopping twenty
and more times at wayside stations not just for the
transfer of passengers to branch lines but to discharge
all manner of merchandise. That we missed a more
important train was due to Holmes's insistence on
purchasing at the station an ordnance survey map of
the county of Oxfordshire, while I supplied myself
with a quarter of a pound of mint humbugs. Invariably,
I find they tranquilize a journey.

I had much need of them. At every halt, we waited
for what seemed an eternity. Crates of ironmongery
and sacks of building materials were delivered and
shunted away. At other stops, corn and potatoes were
taken aboard. The least of the train's aims seemed to
be to reach its destination, which was the village of
Wantage, some two and a half miles from Oxford
itself.

Since that time, fortunately for such as myself, to
whom a visit to Oxford has never ceased to appeal, the

Great Western London-to-Bristol Railway has linked its Oxford connection with the city itself by means of the Wantage Tramway, but no such facility welcomed us on our arrival in the afternoon of that bitter-cold day.

Our penurious circumstances had dictated third-class travel, so we were denied even such amenities as a restaurant carriage and a water closet. Indeed, what the railway advertised so blatantly as "first-class through lavatory carriages" were locked against us. In order to relieve nature, we had to make a manic dash to the public convenience on the platform at Reading. On returning to the train we sat for a quarter of an hour while live chickens were transferred from a farmer's dray.

I used this time to buy two ham sandwiches from the station saloon, only to be informed by Holmes that their content was unacceptable, which required a return visit to the saloon to obtain bread and cheese. It seemed that Holmes had decided upon a diet which must not include meat, reasoning that if vegetarianism was compatible with the strength of a gorilla, it was surely more healthful to man, a conviction he was to put into practise for less than a week, discarding it as he did so many fads over the years.

The discomfort of the journey was additionally increased by Holmes's apparent desire to pass it meditatively, so that he sat on the seat opposite mine, cross-legged in the attitude of an Indian fakir. He maintained that by so doing, the passing scenes of countryside would not deflect him from his concentration on the case in hand. I considered this very unnecessary, in fact quite ostentatious, since it aroused the curiosity of perfect strangers. One countrywoman, alighting at a

rural halt, actually prodded Holmes, to reassure herself that he was in fact alive. Thus for sixty miles of
monotonous travel, punctuated by stops and starts, I
had no socially acceptable fellow traveller to converse
with in a carriage that began to reek of the homespun
smoking mixtures of its horny-handed occupants, simple peasants who nudged one another in amusement at
the spectacle of my eccentric friend.

I have always considered the English railway system to be a microcosm of the class system of the
nation whose barriers one crosses at one's peril. I
would not maintain, of course, that it is necessary to
go the length to which the duke of Marlborough goes in
order to avoid contact with the common man. When
the duke wishes to travel to Oxford from Blenheim
Palace, his ancestral estate at Woodstock, a special
first-class coach is added to the train for him and his
secretary. Businessmen travel second-class, workmen
and farmers third, and goods wagons at the back haul
cattle and coal. That, of course, is segregation taken to
the ultimate, affordable only by the very rich, but I do
agree that if, as some radicals have been predicting,
classes of travel eventually become obsolete and trains
are declared classless, it will be a sorry day for England.

After the journey by train, our ultimate destination
was to be Cragwitch Manor, for evidently the mysterious Chester Cragwitch was a wealthy landowner, although I must say that his unkempt appearance and
furtive manner on the occasion in the attic when I had
so briefly glimpsed him belied such a status. But, as
Holmes pointed out, anyone in the knowledge that he
was the quarry of a gang of murderous thugs might be
excused for not looking at his best. Be that as it may,

after alighting at Wantage, Holmes discerned from his map of the county that the manor was some distance away and on the opposite side of the city. A brisk walk across the countryside was unavoidable, he said, for we had no money to engage a trap. Nor was he discontent that it would be nightfall before we actually got there, reasoning that the cover of darkness might well be to the advantage of two uninvited strangers approaching the residence of so desperate a fellow. We were far from certain of receiving an hospitable welcome. As it transpired, this was an understatement.

I have held a lifelong affection for Oxfordshire, stemming probably from that first encounter with it. It is truly Middle England, the farming basin that lies tranquilly between the industries of Coventry and Birmingham and those of London. Those dark infernos have no echo in its clean hinterland of farms and beechwoods, even though in those times you could still see from beneath the Chiltern Hills the smoke of London drifting through the Goring Gap. Even on that winter day it was a sweet and peaceful landscape whose ploughlands stretched like sheets of glass beneath their bedding of snow, and icicles and hawthorns bowed down the hedgerows.

I would not reveal my feelings to Holmes, who had taken it for granted that a ten-mile hike was exactly to my taste, but secretly I began to enjoy the walk. The dry, cold air and its purity were balm to my jangled nerves. The concerns which had hung so heavily about me since Rathe's ultimatum began to lighten. I had got my second wind.

I have never felt truly at ease in cities. Even during the years at Baker Street, I would at times retreat to the lakes of Cumbria or to a mountain village in the

Swiss Engadine to cure the afflictions of urban life. And so, as we made our way along the lanes and tracks of Oxfordshire, I delighted in the rural sights and sounds, the call of birds flying homeward in formation, the candleglow in the windows of isolated farmsteads, the observable propriety of all that was natural and orderly in man's environment. As we walked through the dying light of that crisp December day, they were reassuring.

With the tail of his topcoat flying, Holmes set a challenging pace. In the shadowy light he looked like a character from a gothic novel. What was this quality in Holmes, I asked myself for the umpteenth time, which set him so apart from ordinary men? One was sometimes ready to credit that he was composed of insubstantial elements, pure energy rather than flesh and blood. He appeared at times to be a figment of the imagination. Of course, every age fashions its supermen after its own needs. I believe I was privileged to perceive in Holmes those qualities which in the passage of time would reach their full flowering. I could not then know that he was destined to become the most perfect reasoning and observing machine of all time, whose deductions would be as swift as intuitions. But I was aware at moments such as this that I was in the presence of an exceptional being. It was only the pettier side of me which viewed him as a college contemporary from whom all my present problems stemmed.

Yet those problems were most vexing. When the Christmas term ended in a few days' time, I would have to go north to explain my predicament to parents expecting to hear only of my progress toward a university place. I would hardly be able to convince them that I had profited from the companionship of a school friend of notable powers and had occupied my time in the pursuit of a cult that worshipped the Egyptian god of the dead! That was hardly a subject for discussion at Christmastime! Now realizing the turn my thoughts were taking, I checked them and fixed my mind upon the benefits I had derived from knowing Holmes, though I must confess that the enumeration of them did not come easily as we pressed on toward the city of dreaming spires.

Over the centuries more able men than I have described their sensations on seeing Oxford for the first time. I think Nathaniel Hawthorne, that allegorical New Englander who had only recently died, was accurate in his notebooks when he wrote of an impression of picturesque decay. "How ancient is the aspect of these college quadrangles," he wrote. "So gnawed by time. So crumbly, so blackened, so grey where they are not black, so quaintly shaped with here a line of battlements and there a row of gables; and here a turret with probably a winding stair inside, and lattice windows with stone mullions and little panes of glass set in lead, and the cloisters with a long arcade looking upon a green or pebbled enclosure." What Hawthorne had seen in 1856 I was now seeing in 1870. Nothing had changed.

The colleges evoked in me, as I believe they do in most of us who have not had the fortune to be a member of the university, a feeling of envy of their academic glories, their secret privileges, their companionships, and easy assumption of superiority. Later on in my life I was to spend a happy year at Harvard, the college which our former colonists founded in Massachusetts in the early seventeenth century. Is the aura of that seat of learning which is two hundred years old noticeably different to that of Oxford which has existed treble the time? Of course it is, but I will not disparage Harvard. It has antiquity too, but it has not become its slave.

A university education was my most cherished wish, and the knowledge that this was in jeopardy struck me sharply as we walked about the Oxford colleges at dusk. I longed to be accepted in the fellowship of such an institution. It gave me little comfort to remind myself that Oxford had expelled the poet Shelley.

Yet there was another side to Oxford. A member of the Anglican clergy in a recent letter to *The Times* pointed out that in this selfsame city there existed factories where child labour was employed. Even at the Oxford University Press, that prestigious publishing house whose special monopoly was the printing of the Bible, the presses were worked from six in the morning to six at night by children aged from twelve to sixteen, with an hour and a half for breakfast, one for dinner, and a half day on Saturday—over a four-and-a-half-year term! What kind of a society was it that overlooked such evil? What extremes of rationalization were required by the ruling class to prevent them from correcting it? No wonder that *Alice in Wonderland* was currently selling so well. When realities are too grim for contemplation, people escape into fantasy. I see no prospect of that changing.

When we left Oxford, night was upon us; we still had four miles to walk. Cragwitch Manor was in country south of the city, a handsome eighteenth-century home surrounded by its own parklands with extensive tree-lined walks and an octagonal pond. We approached the house along a gravel drive bordered by shrubberies, which led to an impressively porticoed entrance. Above this was a terrace all the windows to which were shuttered, save one. From this, a flickering light suggested that a fire blazed within.

We had almost reached the oak door when a gun blast ripped the air, causing us to dive for cover behind one of the stone columns. Whoever was firing was aiming at us. "Go away," a gruff voice called. "Bloody murderers. Go away. Rame Tep will never get me." At the open window stood the man we recognized as Cragwitch. The frightened occupant of the manor was wearing a dressing robe over a nightshirt and held a short-barrelled pocket pistol in one hand. "Go away, you swine, or I'll shoot you!" And he fired at us again.

Holmes got to his feet and raised his arms in a gesture of submission. He called to the terrified man. "Sir, we mean no harm. We are not armed. We are friends of the late professor Waxflatter. May we come in?"

Cragwitch adjusted thick spectacles and peered down. "Yes, I remember you. You chased me at the funeral. Why did you do that? Why are you following me now? There are two of you. Who is the other young scamp?"

"That is Watson," said Holmes. "He is perfectly harmless."

I tried to pull Holmes back under cover. With that firearm in his shaky hand, Cragwitch was really dangerous. Holmes continued to reason with him. "I need your help, Mr. Cragwitch. I want to know why Rame Tep is pursuing you, and why the others died."

Cragwitch thought this over. "Go away," he said

but with less hostility. "It is none of your business."

"The professor was like a father to me," Holmes pleaded. "I want to bring those villains to justice."

So intent was Holmes on this dialogue that he failed to notice, as I had done, a movement in the shrubbery. I had an uneasy feeling that we were not alone. Only the necessity to keep myself under cover prevented a closer look. In any case, it was probably a prowling cat.

Cragwitch, meanwhile, had relented and had decided to admit us. He was no longer at the window. When he reappeared it was at the main door, which he had laboriously unbolted. He was still holding the gun. But there was also relief on his countenance as if the arrival, so unexpectedly, of two schoolboys was a welcome diversion in his state of siege. "Come in and be quick about it," he said.

Holmes told me I could quit my cover. "We are safe, now, Watson. There will be no more firing to-night." But Cragwitch kept his pistol trained on us as he led us up to his study. It was the room through whose window we had seen firelight. Now a great fire in a massive grate provided us with the first warmth we had enjoyed since the start of our journey. It was a blaze sufficient to light the otherwise darkened room. We warmed our limbs in front of it.

The room had cumbersome fireside chairs made of leather, large bureaus, heavy sideboards, and tables. There were bookshelves stuffed with volumes—which a fleeting glance suggested were of interest to a military man—war diaries, biographies of generals, that sort of thing. One morocco-bound set proclaimed itself *The History of the Ottoman Empire*. Dry stuff, I thought, though by this time Cragwitch himself was relaxed and disposed to be friendly. He took a generous swig from a tumbler filled with whisky. A crystal decanter, as well as several glasses that had not been washed, stood on a table by the window. The room was a big man's room, as Cragwitch was over six feet tall and bulky, but it was uncared for, musty, and for years had known no social life. It characterized its occupant; it had gone to seed.

Cragwitch, I surmised, spent most evenings amid its cloying fug, as vigilant as the whisky allowed him to be, waiting for Rame Tep to appear. His tired eyes testified to nights spent wakefully until the light of day brought him the gift of sleep. But why, I wondered, had he dismissed his servants? Had he distrusted them, too?

When we were relaxed, Holmes showed him the painting of the graduation class. "We found it among the professor's papers," he explained.

The effect upon Cragwitch was extraordinary. "My God!" he exclaimed. "Were we ever that young?" I thought I saw a moistening in his fatigued and craggy eyes. "That was painted decades ago."

Before speaking again Holmes waited for the older man to come to terms with the memories the painting had evoked. Then he said: "Can you explain its significance, sir? It cannot be mere coincidence that everyone pictured there except for you has met with sudden death quite recently. Everyone except you, Mr. Cragwitch, is dead."

Cragwitch slowly nodded, put the picture down, and took his whisky glass to the decanter on the window table. He was refilling it when he flinched. He put a hand to his neck to ease a stab of pain. "Bloody insects," he grumbled. "This house needs a darned good clean."

"You see," Holmes was saying, "I know how Rame Tep operate. I tracked them to their temple in the East End of London. But why, Mr. Cragwitch, did they choose as their victims those men in the painting? Why are they after you? What is really behind it? Is it a vendetta? What is the background? Can you tell us?"

Cragwitch drank more whisky but was meditative. Then he looked straight at Holmes. "What is your name?"

"Sherlock Holmes."

"My name is Watson," I said.

"Well, young Mr. Holmes and young Mr. Watson, you have gone to considerable risk and discovered a great deal. You have come a long way to find me. I feel bound to reward you with my story. But I warn you that the knowledge it will impart is dangerous. Rame Tep is a ruthless sect. Do you really want to know how those men in that group came to such a dreadful end and why I live in fear of a similar fate?"

"Please proceed, Mr. Cragwitch," said Holmes.

"Very well, I will."

But hardly had Cragwitch begun to tell us his story than we became alarmed by indications that he had been impregnated by one of Rame Tep's infernal darts. The pain he had complained about while pouring himself whiskey must have been induced by the missive of a fanatic somewhere in the grounds, which drew from me the confession that I had observed movement in the shrubbery while Holmes was pleading for admission to the manor.

But we had no chance to explore, for as a consequence of the mingling of the poison in his system with the large amount of alcohol he had consumed, Cragwitch became extremely aggressive. It was as much as we could do to restrain him.

Under such conditions Cragwitch's story came to us in fits and starts, so to speak, as the crazed man alternated between lucidity and delirium. It was a dramatic tale, but if I were to restrict the reader to his version of it, which at times lacked coherence and at others continuity, he would be denied the impact the story deserves. I have decided, therefore, to give in subsequent chapters a more detailed account of the events which explain the murders of 1870, which I have been able to reconstruct from the diaries of the late Rupert T. Waxflatter that were salvaged from the attic and came into our possession at a later time. Meanwhile, I will conclude this account of that distressing evening at the manor.

The painting, Cragwitch informed us, was the work of an artist of no particular note who had earned small fees by depicting groups of Brompton students in their graduation year. The young men in this group, of which he was one, all came from wealthy families and each had obtained a university place. They were friends and had decided that prior to going up to their universities they would spend some months travelling in Europe. But the weather on the continent that year proved to be so inclement that in search of adventure and sun they decided to go farther. Washed out of the Riviera, they fared no better in Italy and were debating whether to take their bedraggled selves back to England or press on to Algiers, perhaps, or Malta, or even Cairo. They agreed it should be Cairo.

They travelled to Brindisi and boarded there a ship

going to Alexandria from whence they went overland to Cairo. But in the Egyptian capital they found no hotels of a standard acceptable to an English gentleman. After three miserable nights in a hostelry of a most unsalubrious kind, they rented an agreeable villa which became their base for excursions into Cairo, to the Pyramids, and a proposed journey up the Nile.

The wonders of Egypt so beguiled them that they began to conceive a most audacious plan. As a consequence of Napoleon's occupation, which though brief had been extremely influential, Egypt had been exposed to European ideas and enterprise. Tourists were coming in ever increasing numbers, but the country lacked hotels. Why not build one? They formed a consortium, gained the financial backing of their rich families, and commissioned an architect. By bribing numerous government officials, they had their plans approved and with the advantage of cheap labour began work on the foundations.

But what started as an industrial excavation became an archaeological one, for they were soon to discover that they were at work in an ancient burial ground. The tombs of five princesses who had lived during the period of the Middle Kingdom (1785–1580 B.C.) yielded such priceless relics that work on the hotel was halted while these treasures were prepared for transportation to England.

It was not surprising that they provoked local opposition. Over the years there had been ruthless and indiscriminate plunder of Egypt's ancient heritage. Now, thanks to the influence of the French and the inspiration of their Revolution, Egyptians were far more self-aware and conscious of the importance of their culture. Moreover, these tombs had a particular significance to the people of the nearby village who accused the foreign consortium of desecrating a sacred burial ground. Feelings ran high and the Britishers were aware that their lives were in danger. They asked for military protection, which was corruptly provided. Then one night a terrible thing happened.

"You were attacked," said Holmes as Cragwitch poured himself another drink to ease the strain of these recollections.

"No," he replied. "They were attacked."

Some of the soldiers guarding the foreigners got drunk and began fighting with the village people. Houses were set afire and some villagers died in those fires.

All of a sudden Cragwitch's features creased in agony. He began to slap himself as if his clothes were on fire. Then he ran to the window and seemed on the point of jumping out. Holmes rushed to prevent him.

"Fire!" Cragwitch was yelling. "Fire! Help! Fire!"

"It's the drug, Watson," said Holmes. "Quickly, help me hold him down."

"Listen to me," Holmes said to Cragwitch. "You are not on fire. Your name is Chester Cragwitch and you are at home in Cragwitch Manor."

"I am at home in Cragwitch Manor," the scared old man repeated. "My name is Chester Cragwitch and I am at home. . . ." He began to calm down. We relaxed our grip on him. He inspected his hands for burn marks, but of course there were none. "That was terrifyingly real," he said. "Very frightening indeed. What was I saying?"

"The village had been burned to the ground," Holmes prompted.

"Yes, I mustn't forget. I want to pass on this information. It is time everything was known." With more composure he continued his story.

"We were lucky to get out of Egypt with our lives. We sailed from Alexandria and reached England two weeks later. The financial cost had been enormous. My father alone paid out several thousands of pounds. What became of the venture I don't really know but years later a hotel was built on the site. It is called Pharaoh Palace. It has a very fine reputation. In England we went our separate ways. Two of us went to Cambridge, one to Oxford, I believe. I went to Sandhurst, of course, but I think Hallmark chucked the whole idea of university and began some sort of social work in the East End. He landed up in politics, as you probably know. He was a bit of a radical, damned fool. The one member of the group we all kept in touch with was Waxflatter. You see, after university—I think it was Edinburgh—he joined the faculty of our old school. He lived and taught at Brompton. So he represented for us our old alma mater. We all knew where to find him. Over the years he got letters from us all and when I was in London I sometimes visited him."

"What does all this have to do with Rame Tep?" Holmes enquired.

"I am coming to that," Cragwitch said with some annoyance. "About a year after the incident we each received a most alarming communication. I can show it to you." He crossed to a rolltop desk and began to rummage through its disordered contents. "Here it is."

Holmes and I inspected it. "You'll note," Cragwitch continued, "the unusual letterhead. That is the insignia of Rame Tep. Two serpents . . ."

As he spoke the last word he slumped backwards in

his chair and let out a blood-chilling scream. "Oh God!" he cried. "A snake is attacking me! It's enormous. I must kill it." He leapt to his desk, grabbed a paper-knife and lashed the air with it. But his hand seemed to be under the control of an invisible force, which turned the blade on himself. "The snake has encircled my hand," he shouted. "Vile creature! My God, it is going to spring at me!"

Holmes grabbed Cragwitch's hand in the nick of time and tried to wrest the paper-knife from him. The old man was amazingly strong and they fell to the floor, each wrestling for possession of the knife.

"Listen!" Holmes shouted. "Who are you? What is your name? Where were you born?"

Slowly Cragwitch recited to himself the information Holmes had asked for and became calmer. "I am Chester Cragwitch and I was born at . . ." Holmes grabbed the paper-knife, hurled it far from reach, and looked at me with relief. Cragwitch continued his monotonous recital.

"You received this letter, Mr. Cragwitch," said Holmes, showing it to him.

"Oh, yes." Cragwitch seemed quite recovered. "It was from a member of the sect, a vow of ultimate revenge. The writer, I gather, had lost members of his family when the soldiers set the village on fire. The letter promised that no matter how long it took, those deaths would be avenged and that the mummified bodies of the five princesses would symbolically be replaced. You can see the signature for yourselves."

"It looks to me like *Eh Tar*," said Holmes, "which transcribed from Phoenician-Egyptian would mean 'revenge.' "

"Waxflatter's last words," I said.

127

"Very bright, Watson."

Cragwitch was staring at Holmes. "You filthy murderer," he exclaimed suddenly and grabbed Holmes's throat. Hallucinating again, the deranged man was confusing him with his enemy. "You will never get me," he was shouting while trying to strangle Holmes.

"Watson!" Holmes gurgled. "Speak to him! Tell him his name, Watson."

In the heat of the moment I could not remember it.

"Cragwitch," Holmes prompted hoarsely.

"Your name is Chester Cragwitch and the year is . . ." Again I was at a loss for words.

"Eighteen-seventy, you twit!" Holmes rasped with difficulty.

"The year, Mr. Cragwitch, is eighteen-seventy, and if you're not careful you will throttle Holmes."

To my horror he began moving Holmes, still in a stranglehold grip, toward the blazing fire. Soon Holmes was merely inches from the flames and he could hardly breathe. His eyes were bulging. I jumped on Cragwitch but received from him a tremendous blow which sent me reeling. I crashed into a cabinet filled with trophies, which toppled over from the impact.

When I regained consciousness, it took me some time to comprehend the scene that met my eyes. There were several policemen in the room. Cragwitch lay prone at the fireside. Lestrade held Cragwitch's pistol, having knocked the old boy senseless with the butt of it. Holmes, though shaken, was unhurt. It was Lestrade who looked the most dishevelled. He was pale and haggard as if from a recent illness. He proceeded to explain his presence.

"One of those damn thorns of yours stuck to the

palm of my hand," he said. "The hallucinations were horrible. I wanted to do away with myself. It took four of my officers to prevent me hanging myself. But when it was all over, I began to look into your story."

Cragwitch had regained consciousness. With some show of dignity he shook Holmes by the hand. "You probably saved my life, young fellow," he said.

None of my bones were broken, but I felt I had let Holmes down.

"Well, gentlemen," Lestrade said. "I must get on with this business. This is a very rum affair. I have a number of questions to ask you, Mr. Cragwitch." He turned to Holmes. "I must ask you and your chubby little friend to leave." Two policemen escorted us to the door. "By the way," said Lestrade as an afterthought, "I appreciate your getting me started on this case." They closed the door on us.

Over the grounds of Cragwitch Manor dawn was breaking; the landscape was lifeless and forbidding. Holmes blistered with indignation. "He thanked me for getting him started!" he raged. "What impudence, Watson! I have done all the work for him. I gave him all the leads."

In sympathy I put a hand on his shoulder. "Come on, Holmes," I said. "We have a long way to go together, old friend." And we began the trek back to London.

Chapter Ten

WHILE WE WERE IN OXFORDSHIRE, ELIZABETH HAD been diligently at work in the attic at Brompton in pursuance of the task Holmes had set her. In the knowledge that Mrs. Dribb might at any time decide to implement Rathe's instructions to destroy the professor's papers, Elizabeth had employed herself with urgency, sorting out those papers which indicated the direction the professor's research was taking before his untimely death.

In particular, she had been careful to preserve the specifications and sketches relating to his lifelong interest in—indeed his obsession with—the challenge of flight. And although the prototype of the ornithopter, which had so nearly succeeded in maintaining prolonged flight, had been reassembled and was on the roof, some small components of it were still strewn about the attic. These Elizabeth had collected together and covered with a dust sheet.

Sensibly, she had consigned the documents and sketches to my locker, the only safe place that sprang to mind since Holmes no longer had claim to one, and meritoriously, as it transpired, she had included with these the diaries to which I have referred and which enable me to provide a more detailed reconstruction of that fateful year the Brompton graduates spent in Egypt, with such unforeseeable consequences to their later lives.

Visiting Egypt today is a very different proposition from what it was in the year Waxflatter and his friends arrived in Alexandria with no experience of Eastern ways, no outfits suited to the climate, no specific plans, and anticipation of the comforts they had taken for granted in the playgrounds and spas of Europe. Today, of course, we have our Baedekers to prepare and guide us, the convenience of railways (which we British built, I am proud to say), and hotels where the traveller need have no fear of enjoying other than first-class attention. One need not abandon English cooking, as I am told that the steak and kidney pudding served every Friday at the Turf Club in Cairo is delectable. All those amenities, in fact, which a foreign climate renders necessities, are available to the traveller in Egypt today.

This was not so in 1812 when in the month of July our intrepid Bromptonians landed there out of pure whim, it would seem, as their primary aim had been to leave behind them the disagreeable weather they had experienced in Europe.

Waxflatter's journal gives some indication of the cultural shock. On the day after their arrival from a tiring and dusty journey through the delta he wrote this entry in his journal: "It is all very Eastern and strange. Quite unreal. Our hostelry is abominable and smells like a cesspit. In the courtyard which our various rooms surround, household and human waste flows in a turgid stream which the exertions of the servants, sleepy fellows in gallabiers and tarbooshes, fail to wash away with pitchers of water. This morning at breakfast I had the unpleasant suspicion that the man who brought us thick coffee, which was mostly grounds, had just come in from one such flushing operation without a moment's pause to cleanse his hands!''

This unsalubrious place was all that they had been able to find, arriving so late the previous night without prior reservations. Waxflatter expressed the fear that they would all contract cholera before ever glimpsing a pyramid. He went so far as to call the expedition ''foolish and ill-conceived'' and primarily blamed Hallmark, the youngest in the group, who apparently had first muted the idea; ''an incorrigible romantic, much under the influence of Byron'' is how he described him.

But the same entry gives a foretaste of the ability of the country to beguile even the most reluctant visitor. ''Another window of my room,'' he wrote, ''overlooks a garden where I have just seen a veiled lady walking in the midst of a cloud of pigeons. The morning is warm and grave, and black crows caw meditatively in the highest branches of the trees. There are date palms too, their clusters maroon and amber, and from a distant minaret comes a wailing, warning of life's insubstantiality.''

In fact, each visitor would in time and in his individual way be affected by the country which has been called the Mother of the World. For what land has more entitlement to that description? Her amazing

contribution to our civilizations has been acknowl-
edged by scholars and travellers since Herodotus.
Dating back five thousand years, the miracle of Egypt
began with the Old Kingdom of the first pharoahs, who
had the status of gods and enjoyed limitless power.
The cohesion such autocracy provided enabled a civilization to develop that became so intellectually and
technically advanced that it bequeathed to the world
the craft of writing (by means of the hieroglyphic
system), a rational division of time, healing practices
and methods acceptable to medicine today, and moral
and metaphysical religious ideas whose central theme
of "God in Man" the great surviving faiths have made
their own.

Evidence of all this survives in the form of papyruses from the excavated tombs whose contents have
provided us with a vivid means of reconstructing the
daily life and culture of that ancient period, while the
shrines and monuments themselves are tributes to
man's innate striving for endurance beyond his individual, fleeting span. Incidentally, the secret of Egyptian writing, which had been lost since the sixth century, had not been revealed when Waxflatter and his
friends were there, but a contemporary Frenchman,
Jean-François Champollian, soon discovered it, providing us with deeper insights into the Egyptian miracle. "The story of humanity," wrote Pliny the Elder in
the year A.D. 70, "rests on papyrus." And the tools of
the Egyptian scribes were the prototypes of our paper
and pens today.

When the period of pharaonic power declined, successive conquests added to the Egyptian story. These
began with Alexander the Great's defeat of the Per-

sians, which opened up the great period of Helleniza-
tion. After Cleopatra killed herself with a cobra bite at
Alexandria, the country fell to Augustus and for six
centuries was part of the Roman Empire, until the
Arab conquest of the sixth century. In the course of
time came the conquest by Saladin, whose dynasty
was to rule Egypt with splendor and depravity for a
further six centuries, and there followed the periods of
the Mameluke sultans and eventually of the Ottoman
occupation, which began early in the sixteenth century
and continued through to the end of the eighteenth.
Ottoman rule came close to annihilating Egypt's pride
and identity. Her people lost their sense of heritage
amid the corruption and cruelties of their Turkish
masters. Burdened by exploitation, taxed to the hilt,
the fellahin became demoralized and disheartened until, in 1798, something happened to reawaken them and
give them back a sense of history and nationality.
Napoleon landed at Abukir.

The French brought with them academicians whose
responsibility was to inspect and record the pyramids,
obelisks, and other survivals from the period of the
pharaohs. They compiled a detailed picture of Egypt in
ten remarkable volumes which described the country
as it appeared to them during what was destined to be
a brief but influential occupation and charted its history from the beginning of its ancient civilization.

Napoleon, who was thirty-four, recorded his own
impressions of Cairo:

The population of Cairo is considerable, being
estimated at 210,000 inhabitants. The houses are
built very high and the streets made narrow, in

order to obtain shelter from the sun. From the same motive the bazaars, or public markets, are covered with cloth or matting. The Beys have very fine palaces of an oriental architecture, resembling that of India rather than ours. The sheikhs also have very handsome houses.

The okels are great square buildings with very large inner courts, containing whole corporations of merchants. Thus there is the okel of Seur rice, the okel of the merchants of Suez and of Syria. On the outside, and next to the street, they each have a little shop of ten or twelve square feet, in which is the merchant with samples of his goods.

Cairo contains a multitude of the finest mosques in the world; the minarets are rich and numerous. The mosques in general serve for the accommodation of pilgrims, who sleep in them; some of them occasionally contain as many as 3,000 pilgrims. The mosque of Jemilazer [today the university mosque of Al Azhar] is said to be the largest mosque in the East.

These mosques are usually courts, the circuit of which is surrounded by enormous columns supporting terraces; in the interior is found a number of basins and reservoirs of water for drinking and washing. In one quarter called the Franks are a few European families; a certain number of houses may be seen here such as a merchant of thirty thousand or forty thousand livres a year might have in Europe. They are furnished in the European style with chairs and beds. There are Christian churches for the Copts, convents for the Syrian Catholics. There is a vast number of cof-

fee-houses, in which people take coffee, sherbert,
or opium, and converse on public affairs.

Among the customs the French commander found it
difficult to sympathize with was that of buying and
selling slaves, boys of tender age sold to the Beys by
merchants who had purchased them in Circassia and
Africa. After visiting one such slave market attended
by pashas, viziers, sultans, and beys, where youths
were paraded naked, Napoleon ruminated that it
would be a long time before the Egyptians understood
that the soldiers he commanded were not, in fact, his
slaves!

This, then, was the Cairo our travellers saw during
their sojourn in Egypt a little more than a decade later.
And it was, in fact, in one of the houses in the
European section that they installed themselves after
the discomforts of the hostelry. Just as pertinent to
our story is the fact that after the hero of revolutionary
France made his entry into Cairo, he installed himself
in the most sumptuous of the Mameluke palaces, the
palace of Elfy Bey at Ezbekieh (which later became
the site of Shepheard's Hotel), for it was in that
environ that the youthful consortium began work on a
modern hotel with such dire consequences.

Waxflatter was soon to immerse himself in Egyptian
history. His journal reflects a growing absorption with
it. The more he saw of the great burial sites, the more
he became amazed at the technical and inventive
genius of the ancient period. He also respected the
French (an unpopular stance for a Britisher in those
days) for their attempt to transform a country rife with
brigandage, administrative disorder, and epidemics

into one enlightened by European ideas, yet conscious of its ineffable past.

"The more I read of Napoleon's ambitions for the country, I realize he had some good ideas during his three years of supremacy here. Even if he did dream of a French empire in the East he seems to have had the welfare of Egypt at heart. He built roads; he planned boulevards and squares for Cairo on Parisian lines. He went to state occasions in flowing Egyptian robes and attended Moslem prayers. What a perverse fate it was to be driven out by the British after so short a stay. Now we hear that he has reached his nadir this very year outside Moscow, defeated by the Russian winter."

But the British did not last long in the Egypt of the early nineteenth century, either. When they put to sea, they left a young Albanian from the Ottoman army to maneuver himself to power and create a modern Egyptian renaissance. His name was Mohammed Ali; it was he who was ruling Egypt when our young travellers set up residence in Cairo.

Waxflatter's journal describes a visit he made alone by night to the great Sphinx. Setting out on a donkey on the road to Giza, he met parties of tourists, with their guides, returning to the city from a day of sight-seeing. The Europeans, incongruous on camels, regarded him with curiosity, for to go there at nightfall was eccentric if not dangerous; there were thieves on the road. Bobster had thought him mad not to join a regular expedition, as the others had done, and of the group only Hallmark asked to come with him. But he refused. He was determined to see it alone after the last rays of dusk had vanished and the great silhouette of the Sphinx squatted there imperiously, inscrutable guardian of the Pyramids to the north. So as the unearthly beauty of an Egyptian sunset transformed the sand and the sky, he rode on. An entry in his journal suggests that he was rewarded by an experience that was truly metaphysical.

"It is said that the great Sphinx holds a secret," he wrote, "and I felt sure that it was more likely to be revealed to me in the stillness of the night than to a crowd of sketching sightseers. This age-old lion with a human head is an enigma for the Egyptians themselves and a puzzle for the world. No one knows who made it or when. Even Egyptologists can only guess at its history and meaning. Yet its stone eyes have been witness through the millennia to human greed and folly.

"I stood there transfixed, alone but never lonely, for it was as though all the vanished gods of Egypt—Ra, Horus, Isis, Osiris, Anubis, and the rest—had assembled there to join my vigil. Even the City of the Dead on the rocky, sand-locked plateau on three sides of it, where kings and priests and aristocrats are buried, looked in the darkness like a living city, with its burial chambers, mortuary chapels, and priest rooms. The sand drifts which partly covered it looked in the moonlight like waves from a great ocean. Perhaps, as some have sought to prove, this was the site of Atlantis, the city which rose from the sea."

On this and other expeditions he made alone, which the others thought unsociable, Waxflatter's youthful eyes were appreciating Egypt's most enduring gift to the West: the timeless mysticism of her antiquity.

I quote from his journal again:

The solution to the riddle of the Sphinx could be that it was made for the purpose of keeping away evil spirits from the tombs. This theory suggests that it is an emblem of Khepara, the god of immortality. The bedouins of the nearby village at Giza believe that to be so. They claim that the ghosts of the inhabitants of the City of the Dead haunt the region after nightfall.

But the Sphinx, even with the powers invested in it, has been unable to prevent the despoliation and desecration of the sacred treasures it is presumed to be guarding. Except for tombs still unexcavated, of which thankfully there still may be many, you hardly can find one in which the heavy lids of the sarcophaguses have not been laboriously slid aside by robbers who took away the jewels and precious ornaments they contained.

I learn that the looting of tombs began even in pharaonic times when, as the powers of the pharaohs declined, the people rose in anger at the huge cost and ostentation of their rulers' burial practises, for which they paid with their labour. All administrations, it seems to me, finally crumble when they depress the masses beyond endurance, although it can take an unconscionably long time.

Waxflatter's concerns are understandable. The evidence of despoliation was shocking to so scholarly a young man. Over the centuries the tombs had been desecrated by Greek, Roman, and Arab pillagers. The Romans carried away obelisks and large statuary to adorn their cities and the residences of emperors; future imperial masters would do likewise. In Egypt

itself new townships were built from the remains of the
cities of antiquity by developers disinterested in their
historic value to mankind. Wealthy Cairo merchants
removed priceless reliefs and relics from burial
grounds for use as items of decor in their homes.

"Even now," wrote Waxflatter, "I hear that Mohammed Ali is getting the building materials for his
new factories, sugar refineries, and cotton mills from
the temples at Elephantine and Armant. It shocked me
to learn that the Rosetta Stone, which may prove to be
the key to the interpretation of hieroglyphics, was
nearly lost to posterity. It was discovered by mere
chance by a French soldier while his detachment was
quarrying stone to strengthen French defenses against
the British. The soldier considered it to be just a
broken slab of masonry until one of Napoleon's academicians examined it. Even so, it was eventually removed from Egypt—by us British! It seems we bar-
gained for it with the French. It is now in the British
Museum." In another entry he bewails the fact that the
Sphinx itself has been used for target practice by
successive armies.

During his excursions, Waxflatter saw for himself
that the wholesale removal of treasures was still proceeding. Mohammed Ali's policy of "Europeaniza-
tion" was making Egypt more accessible not only to
foreign technicians and men of commerce but to all
manner of enterpreneurs. The British, Fench, Italian,
and German consulates in Cairo employed networks
of agents to scour the country for papyruses and
works of art for despatch to the auction rooms and
museums of their countries. In time Mohammed Ali
would restrict this lawless trade. Meanwhile, practi-
cally every burial site was strewn with pottery shat-

tered and discarded in the search for richer things, hieroglyphic tablets spoiled from ignorance of them, ruined sarcophaguses from which everything had been taken, save the mummified remains of their occupants' entrails.

Now a new menace had arrived in the form of European tourists. Their passion for relic hunting had resulted in new forms of pilferage as they sifted through the sands and rummaged among ravaged sepulchres for souvenirs. "It is as though Egypt's soul is being violated, its ancient wisdom being defiled," wrote the impressionable Waxflatter.

Chapter Eleven

THERE IS AMPLE EVIDENCE IN THE JOURNALS TO SUG-
gest that the seeds of Waxflatter's future inventiveness
were planted in that Egyptian year.

"Who, I wonder," he writes, "first mixed that solution of lamp black, gum, and water to make ink? Think
of the research that brought them such facility with
weights and measures! And what painstaking observation of the heavens they must have undertaken to
create the only rational calender mankind has ever
devised!"

Waxflatter was aware that England was experiencing an industrial revolution and that his country's
influence in the world was increasing all the time, but
the achievements of the Egyptian dynasties enabled
him to put this into better perspective. "People at
home are coming to believe that we have a God-given
mission to 'civilize' less advanced peoples the world
over," he commented, "yet we show little reverence
for the civilizations of the past. We call what we do not
understand primitive and the faiths that preceded ours
pagan. I believe this to be arrogance of a kind we

should not persist in, even should the British Empire last for a thousand years."

What was to become a lifelong interest in aviation may well have begun as he studied the legends of the winged pharaohs. These even predate the classical myth of Icarus, who flew so close to the sun that his wings melted.

"It would surely be surprising," he reflected, "had these sun-and-star worshippers not aspired to reach the sources of their inspiration."

Another member of the group being profoundly influenced by Egypt was Oscar Hallmark; it was not the ancient heritage but the present plight of the people which moved him. Everywhere there was inequality. The fellahin worked for starvation wages in the over-crowded delta and the squalor in the cities was appalling. It troubled this young idealist. "He is a reformer at heart," Waxflatter wrote. "He wants to do something about it. You cannot sit over coffee with him without his making some remark about the sad state of things. I told him that charity begins at home, that there was plenty to remedy in England. I think he took my comment kindly but I do wish he could enjoy himself more.

"He is a curious fellow and I suspect that Cragwitch and Bobster really have begun to dislike him. Bobster has no time for his sensitivities, maintaining that cheap labour is essential both to a prosperous economy like England's and a country like Egypt, bent on recovery. Bobster is a realist, of course.

"Cragwitch, on the other hand, makes fun of Hall-mark's idealism. I heard him say to Hallmark that what Egypt really needed was for the British to take over because we know how to run things. Cragwitch, by the way, is writing a thesis on the military defences of Egypt and the new army Mohammed Ali is creating. I can't help feeling sorry for Hallmark."

Oscar Hallmark was the son of a rich Bristolian whose fortune had been made in the slave trade. The knowledge of the source of his family wealth had created in the young man a conscience burning with outrage and a desire to make amends. There was little doubt in Waxflatter's mind that Oscar's future lay in politics.

There was plenty to justify anger. Cosmopolitan Cairo bore out his belief that under Mohammed Ali, the first leader for six hundred years to govern with virtual independence from Constantinople, the common people were still the underlings. He was particularly moved by what he witnessed when he walked among the Egyptian and European crowds, which ebbed and flowed in the raucous streets of the city.

There were Syrians in baggy trousers, Greeks in white tunics, swarthy bedouins, blue-black Abyssinians, Armenian priests, and the poor, barefooted fellahin in their skullcaps and ragged shirts. One could see barouches full of laughing Europeans, or rich Egyptian merchants on handsome Arab bays. Running ahead of them were slim young native footmen. No person of position travelled without several such running footmen, Hallmark informed Waxflatter. They died young. The pace killed them. To Hallmark that was inhumane.

The position of women in Egypt also dismayed him. They had not begun to be liberated. All he saw, through slits in headdresses, were eyes which turned aside on meeting his. The tradition of the harem was strong, the birthrate really staggering.

In the provinces there were even worse conditions. Mohammed Ali needed money for his schemes of industrialization and irrigation and was employing brutal overseers to gouge more taxes from the fellahin. When a worker fell behind with his taxes, these "umads" would urge him to flee the village, promptly taking over his land.

Mohammed was also raising an army, by forcible recruitment, for campaigns in Arabia and the Sudan. Villagers were marched in chain gangs into barracks, where many died. Rather than let their children be taken off to the army, some families mutilated them, and in Cairo and Alexandria these limbless cripples begged for alms. Slaves were brought in from beyond the southern border, herding into work camps like caged animals, where thousands grieved to death. Those who lived fetched thirty Egyptian pounds on the Cairo market.

As the ambitious ruler tried to transform his country from a province of the dying Ottoman Empire into an independent one with possessions of its own, it was a time of sickening brutality and the fellahin with their sad, earnest eyes suffered and waited.

But this was not the picture Bentley Bobster would have presented. It seemed perfectly logical to him that a backward land depended on resources of cheap labour if it was to launch itself into the nineteenth century. He had no sympathy for those who could not see this, just as he had no time for the radicals in England, the "little Englanders" who made things difficult for those who believed in progress and policies of imperial expansion. Bobster had a keen eye for business and he recognized that Egypt's situation offered a golden opportunity to be first in one particular field.

Between the Esbekiah Gardens and the Nile there was more than a mile of wasteland from which the Pyramids of Giza were a mere thirty miles away. It was Bobster who conceived the notion that a European-style hotel could be built there to cater to the increasing flow of tourists coming to Egypt. For even though these travellers came to marvel at the Pyramids and ponder the secret of the Sphinx, they also required hygiene and efficiency, deep enamel baths, and European standards of comfort in a land where in the season of the khamsin, the hot desert wind, the air became stifling and tempers rose. Moreover, Cairo was on the overland route to India; a modern hotel would profit from both the commercial and tourist trades.

Of course, there had been talk of a canal to link the Mediterranean with the Red Sea. If such a scheme came to fruition it would permit travellers to India to bypass Cairo, but it seemed highly unlikely to Bobster that anything would come of it. The various nations involved would never agree; such was the case when Napoleon's imagination had been fired by the idea: the British opposed the scheme. Bobster was confident that commercial traffic would continue to pass through Cairo undeterred by the period it had to spend in quarantine on arrival at Alexandria.

There was nothing new in the idea of a canal. Across the Isthmus of Suez the pharaohs had built one linking the Nile Valley and Memphis with the Red Sea. It endured for a thousand years until it silted up. The Persians dug it out again and Herodotus records that it took four days to travel the length of it. The Romans dug a more direct canal which joined the Nile quite close to Cairo. After the Arab conquest, a proposal for yet another waterway was abandoned on grounds of military security, and for similar reasons the Ottoman rulers turned down a plan put to them by the Venetians.

There was faint hope of a new canal, Bobster reasoned, while Britain remained so opposed to one. Britain believed it would attract other ambitious nations to her possessions in India. His proposition for a hotel at Esbekiah was wholly viable.

When he mentioned the subject to Waxflatter, the latter was not at all enthusiastic. "There is an oasis on the fringe of the site, and a really fierce tribe of bedouin encamp there from time to time," he wrote in his journal. "They will not take kindly to being disturbed, though I suppose this government would arrange matters if it smelled foreign currency in the air."

Bobster had made influential contacts with government officials and he had talked of the matter to young businessmen, Greeks and Levantines in the main with eyes on debentures and profit; Cairo was full of them. Bobster's idea was that he and his English friends would form a consortium to finance the enterprise, backed by their fathers, and once the enterprise was set in motion they would leave the administration of it to a local group. "If we are to get cash out of our fathers," Waxflatter wryly commented, "it will be a devil of a business persuading mine. His investments are all in India. I don't think he would be keen on the idea."

Cragwitch was in favour of Bobster's plan. Hallmark, they felt, could be persuaded on the grounds

147

that it would create employment. That left Duncan Nesbit. But Nesbit was on the horns of a different dilemma.

This mild-natured son of a Yorkshire vicar had fallen in love with an Anglo-Egyptian girl who lived in Tanta, a cotton town in the delta. She was the daughter of an English cotton grower and his deceased Egyptian wife. It had been love at first sight between this amber-eyed beauty of seventeen and the young Englishman. Yet Nesbit, older by two years, was far less mature in terms of life's vicissitudes, his sheltered existence having consisted of no more than his upbringing in Harrogate, a most respectable spa, and the years he had spent at Brompton, which was not an institution fitted to prepare him for a love affair in the East. Nazli, on the other hand, possessed a Moslem fatalism which had carried her through the dark days of her mother's illness and death with an equanimity not given to peoples of more refined societies.

Her faith taught her to submit, to surrender, to enter into peace with whatever life offered, which was quite easy to do in terms of Duncan. For she loved this gentle youth with hair the colour of sand and eyes that were blue and trusting. He was from her father's country. She had heard about London and had seen pictures of its great buildings; she had not heard of Harrogate but doubtless it had great buildings, too. Yes, she would marry the beautiful Duncan if he proposed to her. And one evening when the sulky twilight of the delta spread across the veranda of her father's house, he did exactly that. "We were quite stupified when he told us," Waxflatter's diary recalls. "We thought he would be the last to get himself engaged. After all, he is going back to be ordained."

But influences other than his attachment to Nazli were affecting Nesbit's nature. The impact of the East had planted seeds of doubt in his mind that Christian England had a monopoly on the virtues it claimed as its own. "Thou shalt have no other gods but me," chimed the Old Testament, but it was becoming clear to the young Englishman that in other times and in other climes men had striven for moral values while worshipping a panoply of gods. However misguided they had been, they sought salvation, moral guidance, and answers to the meaning of existence as passionately, and about as effectively, as the devotees of the contemporary Christian church.

Naturally, given his theological interests, the focus of his enquiries during his stay in Egypt had been the ancient Egyptian religions with their multiplicity of gods. They dated back to prehistory when gods and goddesses in animal form were the deities of the tribes which first began to cultivate the lands of the delta. Cats and monkeys, vultures and falcons, the ibis and the owl were among the creatures they deified.

As the tribes concentrated into communities and formed cities, many of these gods were embodied into a single all-powerful One, and the idea of a universal God emerged with the sun as Creator.

This concept is enshrined in the ancient Egyptian Books of Wisdom, which are as old as the Pyramids. The concern of these texts is the path of life—the Way. They affirm that men are created equal and they teach a moral system. For the first time God is not blamed for man's afflictions; man himself is responsible for his evil ways.

Egypt thus produced the first concept of monotheism, the idea of one almighty, transcendent deity, the notion of God in Man. A sense of sin, the need for repentance, and the concept of redemption were essences of this theology.

Nesbit realized that the Bible's Book of Proverbs had much in common with ancient Egypt's collection of wise sayings, that the Hymn to the Sun, written in the first millennium before Christ, may well have inspired the Christian psalmists. There were many other examples of Christianity's debt to the pioneering theology of its Egyptian forbears. Yet in one incredible, authoritarian generalization, his own church preached that all other faiths were heathen. This was as disturbing to Duncan Nesbit as the news of his engagement to Nazli was to his father.

Letters from home appealed to the young Englishman, who by nature was conservative and reserved, to think again, to consider the feelings of his family. England had so much to offer, his father reminded him, and Duncan was too young to know his own mind. Besides, it would be unfair to bring an Egyptian girl, even one with an English father, into Harrogate society whose acceptance of her would be a very slow affair. There were some wonderful girls at home; he had his education to think about. Duncan's father implored his son to take his time before marrying. Finding the mental conflict difficult to contend with, Nesbit confided in the member of the group for whom he had most respect.

"He is very vulnerable to the criticism he is receiving from his father," Waxflatter wrote. "He would have been far wiser to keep the matter to himself for a while. He has even written, it seems, about the scheme to build the hotel. The vicar has condemned that, too. I think he simply wants his son out of Tanta and back home. There is no money on the father's side; it is apparently all with the mother. If Nesbit does come into Bobster's group, where is he going to get the money?"

But Nesbit did join the consortium. If he could not take Nazli back to England without creating social ill-feeling, he would have to stay in Egypt and he would need a source of income. He spoke to Nazli on the subject. She discussed it with her father. When Nesbit came into the consortium it was with Nazli's father's backing.

That left Hallmark and Waxflatter undecided but, as Cragwitch had predicted, the former was susceptible to the belief that the enterprise would bring work to the region, and prosperity to some of the hard-pressed fellahin. This had a potent appeal for Hallmark. What more appropriate way was there of returning some of his family's ill-gotten wealth to the exploited and oppressed? It was a naive concept, of course, but one of which neither Bobster nor Cragwitch saw fit to delude him. He joined the consortium, leaving only Waxflatter to make up his mind. How that came about, and with what result, is recorded in Waxflatter's journal.

"Immediately after breakfast today Bobster called us all to a meeting," he records. "Hallmark rather shocked us by turning up in Arab robes and a turbanned fez. Cragwitch was particularly sour to him and muttered something about Oscar going native. Nesbit came in from Tanta looking rather pleased with himself, I am glad to say. Anyway, the point of the meeting was the hotel scheme; it seems that for one reason or another they are all pretty game for it. Was I game too? they wanted to know. Well, I asked for more time to make my decision. I have given a lot of thought to it, of course, and there are pros and cons. Although I'm not a businessman, I see that the time is ripe for a hotel in that position. But do I want all the bother? That's the kernel of the matter for me, at any rate."

Some days later, Bobster was impatiently demanding a decision from the equivocating Waxflatter. Surprisingly, he got one; Waxflatter had decided to join the consortium. From random entries made before the foundation work actually started, one could assess the reasoning which led to Waxflatter's decision. It was to do with his ambition to go into teaching after university.

"I cannot hope to earn a fortune as a teacher," he confided to his journal. "I will need something to bring me in reserves. Especially as I want to do research of my own. Neither an academic grant nor government money is likely to be given for research in the area I have in mind—the top people in England simply do not believe in it—so I must look elsewhere for support. An income from the hotel could be the solution."

In this frame of mind he wrote to his father, a gentleman farmer in Somerset, proposing that monies in trust for him be released; in two years' time they would be his by right, anyway. His father, who had harboured misgivings concerning his son ever since the impetuous boy had leapt from the top of a silo wearing homemade wings, quickly agreed to the proposal on condition that he would never ask for more. Waxflatter, therefore, was able to invest with the others in the consortium in the knowledge that if it suceeded—and Bobster was very astute—he would have the finance for independent research.

From what we know of Waxflatter we can have little doubt that the area of research in which he intended to work was aviation. We have other evidence of that. A thesis he had written at about this time was also among the memorabilia Elizabeth removed to safety from the attic. It is a fascinating document, a gem of its kind, a pastiche which traces the history of flight from the dreams of the ancients through the achievements of his own day.

Man's abiding desire to defy gravity and take to the air, which Waxflatter himself would embrace with dedication during his years at Brompton, is charted from misty antiquity. Indeed, flying gods were so numerous that he was led to make the daring suggestion that the very seeds of man on Earth might have been planted by visitors from other planets. He delineated the devices which from the earliest times had used the properties of air—the boomerang, the feathered arrow, the windmill, and the kite. The man-bearing kites of China a thousand years before Christ are mentioned. So are rockets invented in the same age. He anticipated machines which, by combining the properties of the kite with the windmill, or the windmill with the rocket, might one day propel man into the atmosphere or even beyond.

Tribute is given to Leonardo da Vinci's work at the close of the fifteenth century, particularly to his designs for flapping-winged ornithopters. As we know, da Vinci's principles were applied to the flying machines Waxflatter later built himself. Remembered too in the thesis are the worthy, winged eccentrics who across the centuries hurled themselves off towers, from steeples, and across battlements with injurious

and sometimes fatal consequences—men like Oliver of
Malmesbury who took wing from the roof of the
Abbey, breaking both his legs (1020), De Bernoin of
Germany, who in Frankfurt killed himself in a similar
attempt (1673), and the Marquis of Bacqueville, who
tried to wing his way across the Seine and crashed
onto a washerwoman's barge (1742). Waxflatter pays
respectful credit to these heroic misadventures before
moving on to the balloonists of the eighteenth and
early nineteenth centuries, the dirigibles, and finally,
to the first true aircraft with propulsive flappers which
in his own day he would endeavour to perfect.

This was the worthy obsession which led Waxflatter
to join the consortium. With everyone now in accord,
Bobster lost no time in getting the project started. But
he could go no faster than the customs and the character of the country allowed. There were inevitable
delays, the reasons for which, in Eastern lands, are
never made particularly clear and the blame for which
cannot ever be precisely apportioned. Officials refused
to be hurried, bargains had to be made, the climate
was inconducive to pressure, and the days passed in
the leisurely observance of the siesta. Soon it was
clear that it would be months before work could begin
on the foundations of the new hotel.

Except for Bobster, who remained in Cairo at the
pivot of things, the friends temporarily dispersed.
Nesbit lulled time away in Tanta, Cragwitch went
north to Alexandria to study the remains of the Napoleonic fortifications, Hallmark rented rooms in the
native quarter and studied Arabic, and Waxflatter
began a journey up the Nile.

It was undoubtedly an unhappy omen that when the
time came for the work to be started, the bedouins

began moving into their encampment at the oasis near Esbekiah to observe the month of Ramadan. One night in that month, the ninth of the Muslim year, is called the Night of Destiny. During that night the fates of men are fixed for the coming year—and, as it would transpire in the cases of the young Englishmen, for a time considerably longer.

Chapter Twelve

WAXFLATTER'S PLAN TO SAIL UP THE NILE RIVER TO the first cataract was to be thwarted. Early on, problems arose which he had not anticipated. After a good start from Boulak on a brilliant afternoon with a fair breeze, the crew of the flat-bottomed, two-masted barge he had hired for the journey became churlish and demanded more pay, a tactic that was not uncommon after the start of such a voyage. Then unseasonal winds twice put the boat aground, the second time so seriously that they had to go ashore. He was forced to stay the night in a village at Turra comfortlessly billeted in a mud hut with his six crewmen, a dragoman, and a cook. The village was on the road to Memphis and so he decided to visit that famous city while the crew got the ship afloat again.

With his dragoman he set off on the long journey by donkey across the desolate sands, but on reaching the famous ruins, a messenger from Cairo caught up with them. Bobster was anxious for his early return.

Work on the project would start sooner than expected. All difficulties had been solved except for some minor disagreements with the elders at a village near the site. Waxflatter thought this sounded ominous, though Bobster was not of a mind to think it serious. "Relative to these localized problems," he had written, "I am quite confident that Hallmark will sort them out. He will be our liaison. Already he has some Arabic and judging from appearances he is part way to becoming an Arab himself! I feel strongly we should all be there for the start of the work on the foundations. I think you will see the importance of showing the flag."

The journal bristles with irritation. "Damn Bobster's bloody flag-waving!" Waxflatter wrote in his journal. "What had that to do with a business venture? I have supported it with my money. What else can I do? Bobster has a better business head than the rest of us put together. I want to see Abydos and the Valley of the Kings. I may never get another chance."

By the following day his ill-humour had quelled. "It's a damnable shame and all that, but I suppose I had best turn 'round. If something goes wrong, the absentees will take the blame for it. I want this venture to succeed. I need the independence it will provide, so after a day at Memphis I'll go back." He could not help reflecting on the irony of Bobster's remarks concerning Hallmark, whom he and Cragwitch had so often ridiculed. Now he was to come into his own as their liaison officer. "Good for Hallmark," he wrote. "Trust they will show him more respect in future."

Carrying as a guide his Herodotus (the Greek historian had ventured there in the fifth century B.C.), Waxflatter reached Memphis anticipating with excitement his first sight of the remains of a city founded four thousand years ago. But arrival brought disillusion, for all that was left of what had been Egypt's capital through thirty-one dynasties, a city that had survived through the Persian, Greek, and Roman conquests and was still populous when the Arabs came, were huge mounds of dusty earth. Here and there palm trees grew, goats struggled for existence in their shade, and beyond the trees were mud huts outside of which women and children sat disconsolately in the heat of the day.

Nothing remained of the splendours Herodotus had seen but fragments of granite sculpture, headless torsos and a colossus lying face down in a dried-up lake. "The ruins have sunk into the fathomless sands," Waxflatter wrote in his journal. "Memphis is a disappointment. One is drawn here by the name." Nevertheless, he had a sense of history as he wandered over the desolate mounds, picking up here a bit of porcelain, there a fragment of red granite. This was hardly surprising, for the vanished Memphis had been the world's most ancient city. No city had prospered for so long a period after its founding by Khufu, whom the Greeks call Cheops in their histories. "All sunk into an ocean of sand," he wrote regretfully. Of course, he was wrong. We know now that it was man and not the sands that claimed the ruins. The splendour Herodotus had seen had been carted off in the Middle Ages to build new cities. Some of Cairo is built from the masonry of Memphis.

Leaving the forlorn place, Waxflatter rationalized his feelings. He immersed his disappointment in the satisfaction of having been there and having seen what little still remained. In this frame of mind he began the donkey ride back to Turra with his dragoman.

During the river trip to Boulak he was already dreading what he might find in Cairo. "I don't like the sound of this business with the bedouin," he confided to his diary. "I can only hope that Bobster knows what he's about."

On arrival, he found that the situation was even worse than he had feared. Not that Bobster thought it so; what had occurred appeared to give Bobster great satisfaction.

The site proposed for the hotel had turned out to be an ancient burial ground. Already many priceless treasures had been retrieved from it. "We are millionaires before we even start," Bobster told the others with immense delight. It was Hallmark who sobered their thinking. Returning from a meeting with the village elders, he informed his friends that the matter was extremely delicate. The site they were excavating was regarded by the villagers as sacred. Five princesses of the fourteenth dynasty were buried there. Waxflatter decided to visit the village near the site. He was accompanied by Hallmark.

Before they set off, Waxflatter was shown a brochure produced for the consortium; it described the amenities to be offered by the hotel. From extracts he included in his journal we can see that the hotel would have been truly magnificent, a grand hotel blending the latest in American technology with the ambience of the East.

An American architect had executed the design. At that time America was pioneering the field, building luxury hotels which attempted to equal the splendour of Europe's royal palaces of which, of course, they had none. It was in America that hotels were first built in advance of the tradition of the English inn, where travellers stayed overnight only if they had to. The new trend was toward hotels as social centres, fantasy worlds where visitors were cosseted as if they were kings. Hotels of this quality were opening up in Europe too, several of them being conversions from palaces and castles, even monasteries and convents. If one was sufficiently well-off, one could enjoy at the recently completed Exchange Hotel in Boston or the Badischer Hof at Baden-Baden a complete break from the cares of every day in the utmost luxury. It was a hotel of this concept that the architect had designed for the consortium in Cairo.

It would be six storeys high with one hundred and fifty apartments, each containing a water closet, which was quite revolutionary. The complex would include a dining room seating two hundred persons from the terrace of which there was a view of the Nile. This would be called the Salon of the Dynasties. There would be a ballroom, a library, an Arabian Room equipped to show kaleidoscopic lantern shows, a bathing establishment complete with Turkish steam baths and massage rooms. A very special feature would be the Gateway to India, which the promoters described as a reconstruction on theatrical lines of a market where Egyptian artifacts might be purchased in far more comfortable surroundings than in the rowdy, restless alleyways of the native bazaars of Cairo.

The entire edifice, in red granite, was designed to blend in with the landscape: mosquelike columns, crowned with minarets, standing on each side of a central entrance facade which was triangular, like one side of a pyramid. The hotel would be called, in poor taste, Waxflatter thought, the Pharoah's Palace.

They went to the village on horseback and Waxflatter mentioned the panache with which Hallmark, in Egyptian costume, rode his Arab steed; he had become remarkably Egyptianized. One would not have recognized the former public schoolboy in his burnous and red flat-topped cap above stubbled, sunburned features. On arrival, Waxflatter felt conspicuous as the only one in European attire, but Hallmark evidently had gained the confidence of the villagers and they were invited to take refreshment in the hut used by the council of elders. He describes the occasion:

"I was impressed with the scrupulous good manners of these men—whose lives were so hard and menial—and with the cleanliness of their dwelling with its bare, earthen floor. We sat on finely woven cushions in a half-circle, with their spokesman in the middle. Bowls were passed around in which we cleansed our hands before partaking of the sweets and coffee offered by children whose smiling brown eyes were the sole part of their anatomy visible through slits in their black, ground-length robes. From a peephole in a curtain that divided us from an adjoining room, a succession of bright eyes watched us furtively and we heard the light, gleeful laughter of the women in the seclusion of purdah. The simplicity of it moved me deeply."

The problem, the chief said, was that the site for the proposed building was hallowed ground to them. What appeared to the Europeans as wasteland was territory they and their forefathers venerated, for beneath it, undisturbed for thousands of years, lay the tombs of Princess Hatiba and her four sisters who, ancient texts recorded, had all died in one terrible night of catastrophe when the Nile had risen before its timely season and had devastated the imperial residence. Many died through drowning, among them the five royal heirs.

Each year during Ramadan, on the night before the Day of Destiny, the village solemnly marked that sad event of antiquity with a torchlit vigil at the entrance to the tombs.

The chief continued his narrative in rather sterner tones. He told the Englishmen, addressing Hallmark in particular, as translator, that the young men from Europe and the moneylenders from the city (he used the Arabic word for usurers) had begun to disturb this hallowed ground and were unbending when asked to stop their sacrilegious work. The chief, therefore, demanded that the defilement of the tombs cease at once.

"There was in his manner a cool civility whose very tone warned us not to mistake it for weakness," Waxflatter commented in his journal. "And they have pointed to a further complication. A tribe of bedouin, with whom they have close and amicable ties, is encamping at a nearby escarpment in preparation for Ramadan. They too have seen what is happening at the holy ground. 'We use peaceful means of persuasion in matters of this kind,' said the elder, 'but our brothers of that tribe do not. Their ancestry goes back unfathomable centuries (the old chief actually said 'to the time when Ram was omnipotent,' but Hallmark could not precisely translate) and to belief in the cult of Rame Tep. Even to this day they embalm their dead in reverence to Anubis, the god of the dead, and in the season of Ramadan bury the remains of their loved ones at the tombs of the five princesses. If the tombs are defiled they will evoke the vengeance of Eh Tar.' "

All this sounded ominous to Waxflatter and quite

naturally he wanted to know more about the significance of Eh Tar. Hallmark explained that from each generation this particular tribe chose one male child ('the chosen one,' usually the son of the tribal chief) and gave him the name Eh Tar. If the need arose, this princeling was their "messenger of revenge"; *Eh Tar,* traced back to the Phoenician, actually meant revenge. Whoever defiled the tombs of the princesses would finally have to answer to the vengeance of Rame Tep whose messenger would be Eh Tar.

Somewhat shaken by these revelations, Waxflatter suggested to Hallmark that they should now visit the building site. En route to it, Hallmark told him what else he had learned about the culture and customs of the desert tribes.

The bedouin, or Bedu of Arabia, were the nomadic camel-breeding tribes and, strictly speaking, they alone were entitled to be called Arabs. These tribesmen pursued a wandering existence even in pharaonic times. When they migrated from Arabia to Egypt, they still lived nomadic lives and were spoken of by Egyptians as Arabs, whereas those who cultivated the land or lived in cities were not. But in recent years there had been some settling by the tribes, several of which had given up the terrible hardships of their desert lifestyle to become peasant farmers, usually in conjunction with villagers already established as growers or keepers of cattle. This trend had been accelerated by the Napoleonic occupation, which had brought with it notions of equality and fraternity inspired by the French Revolution. Some tribesmen even had joined with village fellahin in a migration to the cities where they were employed as labourers in new schemes of urbanization and industrialization. But eventually as a sense of Arab nationalism arose, all Arab-speaking peoples were referred to collectively as Arabs.

Yet the bedouins were the historic thoroughbreds of their race and most of the tribes remained nomadic, eking out an existence in the intense heat and cold of the arid desert regions of southern Arabia, the least hospitable of which was the infamous Empty Quarter. Yet they were fiercely patriotic, and over the centuries successive rulers had called upon them to fend off the incursions of intruders, from the Christian crusaders to the present, when Mohammed Ali had not hesitated to use them to chase away the British.

The bedouins encamped near the village at Ezbekiah were typical of a tribe in transition. They owned some emaciated cattle, they had a few camels, and they possessed a herd of goats. They were small, wiry men with fine features and lean bodies, but even their youths seemed older, due to the harshness of their lives. They wore head cloths and Arab shirts which reached halfway down their calves, though some wore only loincloths and were bareheaded. They wore daggers, too. Their women, in black, tended the cattle but were not allowed to milk them; from antiquity, only a man was allowed to touch an animal's udder. But it was the camel which filled the role of universal provider. This splendid beast of burden provided their transport, their meat in the hardest of times, milk, and by means of its dried dung, their fuel for cooking and heating. Naturally, they revered the camel, admiring its patience and treating it with a blend of affection and practicality that almost amounted to love. For should a travelling tribe be within riding distance of a much-needed oasis and the camels in need of rest, they would proceed no farther nor spend another night in the inhospitable desert.

The bedouins' lives were sheer hardship. Wells were sometimes so bitter that they mixed camel milk with it to make it drinkable. They were plagued by heat sores when the khamsin blew its furnacelike wind from the east. For such tribes, life was so close to nature, so troubled by difficulties of existence, that God was a companion; faith in His presence gave them courage to endure. They prayed regularly, facing Mecca on their prayer mats, and observed Ramadan as a movable feast since, according to the Egyptian lunar calendar, it falls eleven days earlier each year.

A man may not eat or drink from dawn to dusk during Ramadan but so hard is a bedouin's lifestyle that such a routine would be fatal in the desert heat. So a bedouin was allowed the exemption of observing the fast when he had ended a journey.

Such was the situation of the tribe that had encamped on the escarpment near Esbekiah. They had spent part of the year in caves in limestone cliffs, they had crossed the Empty Quarter, and now they had moved down to the oasis where they had spread their tents and built huts of stones and matted grass in which to house their few possessions. But at night Waxflatter and his friends could hear the beat of their high-pitched silver drums tapping out the hours of nightfall when they modestly ate and drank between the daytime fastings. It was like a warning to the Europeans, tapping away the time to Ramadan when, as Hallmark warned, these tribesmen would come down to the burial ground to join the village people in a night of vigil before the Day of Destiny.

Waxflatter's next concern was to inspect the building site to assess how much had so far been done that was likely to affront the bedouins' sensitivities. He could not have been more appalled by what he found on reaching the plateau designated as the site for Pharoah's Palace.

A force of labourers comprising some one hundred and fifty, all of them fellahin, was at work there, but the nature of their toil appeared to have scant relation to the construction of a hotel. Earthworks had been started, supposedly for the foundations, but what was in progress gave the impression of being no less than plunder. While carpenters were making posts and slats to shore up exposed caves and passageways, other labourers were digging deeper into the earthworks. Others still were constructing crates of various sizes and lining them with straw and other padding materials.

From the caves to the crates moved a traffic of workmen carrying statuary and ornaments; perfectly intact sarcophaguses were being transported shoulder-high. At first glance, these looked colourless, until one noticed, as the rays of the sun touched them, the subtle colours of their varnishes. Strewn about the site like rubble were bits of what had once been elegant vases, fragments of alabaster, and marble of every hue, from dazzling primaries to muted pastel shades. Funeral statuettes had been callously discarded as imperfect, their limbs and headless torsos tossed about the place as if by an explosion. More appalling still, there were brown lumps of a spongy substance protruding from tattered burial shrouds. This was the flesh of broken mummies. It was like a charnel house.

Waxflatter recorded that this vandalism was proceeding under the watchful eyes of persons he had never seen before; none had been at meetings when the hotel project was discussed. Later he would learn that these unsmiling men in business suits were agents of foreign consulates, dealers in antiques, go-betweens from European museums. Bobster, it seemed, had made a deal with them in the name of the consortium, whereby sums of money would be paid toward the cost of construction after these priceless relics had been sold.

In the absence of the others, Waxflatter had been outwitted by these ruthless entrepreneurs, outclassed by their corrupt double-dealing. Now he was hopelessly in their power. Hallmark, almost speechless with anger, sternly warned of the dire consequences, but Cragwitch discounted the risks, claiming influence with the military, who would certainly provide troops to protect them in the event of any trouble. The politicians in Cairo needed money for their ambitious plans for renewal, he said, and it would be the simplest thing in the world to siphon some of the profits their way. Only Nesbit, recalled from his tryst in Tanta, seemed impervious to these tensions. He was eager to see inside the excavations, an expedition in which the others joined.

The five princesses had been entombed some four thousand years before, mummified, and placed in a sepulchral temple guarded by a pair of small sphinxes. By the light of hand-held candles, they threaded their way along an avenue of catacombs and on reaching the inner temple their escort lit a pan of magnesium. The flare revealed the incredible richness of it all to them. Recesses shone with gems, reliefs in polished ivory depicted the profiles of gods and goddesses, hieroglyphic tablets proclaimed the wisdom of the Book of the Dead. And on tableaus inlaid in gold were the sarcophaguses of the five princesses. But they were empty. The mummies had been removed.

Some fifty yards farther on they came upon a chamber which Hallmark identified as an embalming house. Here the funeral rites had been enacted those many millenia ago. He had some knowledge of this long-lost art, which he proceeded to share with his friends.

First the corpse was emptied of all corruptible materials and packed in natron. Only the heart was left, the entrails being preserved separately in canopic jars for burial with the body. The corpse, once dried, was washed, oiled, wrapped with linen bandages, and handed over to the relatives. Now the actual funeral could begin, a quite festive affair that usually ended with dancing. The departed one was then assumed to have joined the community of its ancestors. In the case of royalty, such as the burial of the princesses, the ceremony would have lasted several days and the burial ground would have become a place of pilgrimage.

"Standing there in that cold underground temple," Waxflatter confided to his journal, "I felt I was more than just an intruder into the private world of an ancient faith. I had offended the strict laws of time. Perhaps now these hallowed dead would never awaken. I had broken the spell. I suppose that is the meaning of sacrilege."

By the time the five young Englishmen returned to their villa in Cairo they were seriously at loggerheads. From the journal we receive the distinct impression that Waxflatter wanted simply to return home. For his part, Hallmark was so disgusted by the defilement taking place at Esbekiah that he felt unable any longer to face the village people. Nesbit was keen to return to Tanta. But both Bobster and Cragwitch insisted that they all should stay until the building work had started and the project could safely be left to their Egyptian associates. But all this was to prove pointless conjecture because on the following day there occurred a series of events which would lead to their departure for England at the earliest opportunity and by the fastest means.

Cragwitch had arranged for a contingent of the military to guard the excavation. These soldiers were Albanians, veterans of Mohammed Ali's notorious adventures in the Sudan; a crueller bunch of mercenaries would have been impossible to find. When, on the eve of the Day of Destiny, the villagers, followed by bedouins on camels, approached the holy site, the soldiers shouted lewdly to their women. They had been drinking from beer kegs set up on the sawed-off stumps of cedar trees. The Arabs were confused and angry, for not only had the hallowed Muslim shrine been hideously defiled but at this solemn time was being guarded by infidels.

Daggers were drawn by the bedouins and shots were fired by the Albanians. Skirmishes began and the Arabs retreated to the village. After nightfall, the Albanian soldiers pursued them and all hell broke loose. Homes were set afire, women were raped, unspeakable cruelties were perpetrated. By dawn, the village was a ruin. An acrid smoke wafted across the prone bodies. Some were merely sleeping off their drunkenness, some were crying from their wounds, but many, including children, were dead or dying.

News of the outrage reached the villa soon after dawn, brought to the Englishmen by one of Bobster's friends, a Greek from Alexandria. "I would advise you all to leave without delay," he told them. "There is hatred for foreigners among the survivors. The government will turn against you, too. They will not take the blame. You will be named as the culprits."

"Which is what we are," Waxflatter confessed to the pages of his journal, adding prophetically, "we may not have heard the last of this."

By evening they had reached Alexandria, where they were lucky to get passages on a ship leaving that night for Liverpool. None of them would ever return.

However, we know something about the careers they followed. The evidence is in the diaries Waxflatter kept through the years.

Hallmark did much good work in the slums of London's East End. He knew Charles Dickens quite well. He published a novel of his own, *The Lanes of Evil,* which did much to make the authorities build better housing in the impoverished neighborhoods of the dockland. Eventually he was to enter Parliament—as a radical, of course.

Nesbit, who had been forced to leave Egypt without the opportunity of bidding farewell to his loved one, on returning home, had a change of heart, greatly to the relief of his family. After his ordination he served the flocks of several parishes before settling in at Kilburn for what would prove to be the remainder of his life.

Bobster, as we have seen, died spectacularly, at the peak of his prosperity. It emerged much later that when a hotel was eventually built at Esbekiah, he managed to have shares in it, probably under another name or through a holding company or by some other means known to an accountant. By managing the financial affairs of others, he had become a very rich man, indeéd.

After a short military career rumoured to have ended under a cloud (he shot an Indian, instead of a bird, during a pigeon shoot in Delhi), Cragwitch retired from the army and went into merchant banking. He would be the sole survivor of the 1870 murders.

Waxflatter, as we know, returned to his old school after graduating from Edinburgh. It would seen that he accepted the place at Brompton largely because he was offered space there to undertake practical experiments of his own in the field of aeronautics. He was not interested in money. All he wanted to do was to fly.

Chapter Thirteen

FOLLOWERS OF THE HOLMES ADVENTURES WILL know that by profession I am a physician, for I did achieve that status, despite the fears that plagued me when I was at Brompton. I have never claimed for myself conspicuous talent as a writer. The durable nature of the Holmes casebooks, I am the first to concede, has not been attributable to whatever expertise I may, or may not, possess as their narrator. No, their success has been due to the degree of admiration they have aroused in the public mind for the amazing achievements of their central character, my friend Holmes.

I know that on more than one occasion—I am thinking of the case of "The Musgrave Ritual"—he referred to me as his biographer. With that authority I gave myself the same appellation while recounting the case of "The Resident Patient." And during his investigations into the riddle of "The Norwood Builder" he went so far as to describe me as "my zealous historian." But I have never harboured any illusions as to the quality of my penmanship. My work must be seen as that of an amateur, dedicated, but an amateur all the same, just as in the field of detection Holmes is an amateur, albeit a supremely gifted one.

At times, however, he could be woundingly critical of my efforts to provide posterity with a record of his work. More than once did he accuse me of "embellishment"—his very word—in the course of my self-imposed task of relating what he chose to call "these little records of our cases which you have been good enough to draw up." Well, I could contend with the patronizing nature of his opinion but I felt very deeply the injustice of the charge he made while we were attempting to solve the mystery of "The Copper Beeches" to the effect that I had "degraded what should have been a course in logic into a series of tales."

Such belittling phraseology I considered unworthy of his professed regard for me. Had he not described me, during our enquiries into "The Red-Headed League," as "my partner and my helper"? Yet notwithstanding this regard, he could lecture me most severely upon my literary shortcomings when he was not in a sweet temper.

Why, the reader may ask, am I reminded of this? Essentially because I can feel his presence now as I write in my study in Kensington, his shadow lurking between the lamplight and my desk. He is leaning over my shoulder and I swear I hear him say, "Watson, old friend. You have embellished again."

In my mind I deny the charge, although I am aware that it has some substance from the point of view of Holmes. He is upbraiding me for having lingered in Egypt, for having detailed those events at the cost of abandoning him to the wilds of Oxfordshire and Eliza-

beth to her toils in the attic. That is typical of Holmes.
For him the chase is everything. The state of the world
in general has never interested him; the subject is
boring. "My life," he once said to me, "is one long
effort to escape the commonplace of existence." It
was a battle with ennui. Yet here was a man whose
intuitions were so uncanny that had he lived in the
Middle Ages he might well have been accused of
witchcraft and summarily burnt at the stake!

But I make no apology for having used the rich
source of the Waxflatter diaries to detail what happened in Egypt. Was there ever a more classic case of
the fate of individuals being determined by the inexo-
rable course of history? It was because those young
people in the painting had been in a particular place at
a particular time that their lives were lived under the
stress of a threat of vengeance they received a year
after their return. Had not history coagulated in that
night of carnage at Esbekiah, I would not now be
relating Holmes's very first case. But I take his point.
It is time to return to Brompton.

Unknown to us while we were at Cragwitch Manor,
Elizabeth's very life was in danger. Just how perilous
was her plight we would not discover until our return
from Oxfordshire. Then it would be almost too late. In
due course I was able to piece together the details of
those terrible hours she endured.

When we left for the manor she went to the attic as
Holmes had directed. There she began the unenviable
task of sorting through her uncle's paraphernalia. She
packed the prototypes of his more portable inventions
in shoe boxes. These included a clockwork egg slicer
he had long meant to patent; a device governed by a
spring which turned the pages of a book with a built-in

timer one could set in accordance with one's reading pace; and a bedside coffeemaker, which had little chance of meeting safety standards since it was fuelled by gas! Along with one or two more of her uncle's gadgets, these items seemed in her opinion to show the ingenuity of his mind to best advantage. So with various documents and the diaries, she conveyed them to my locker.

Several stealthy journeys were required until morning light made further trips inadvisable, due to the risk of discovery. It was amazing just how much she managed to cram into a locker already housing my football socks, two novels (one by Wilkie Collins, the other by Thackeray) and a half-pound of Rowntree toffees, bursting from the bag. The scientific world certainly would be poorer had she not managed to include among the papers Waxflatter's designs for an ornithopter, powered by steam, an advance on the pedal-powered version. Although he did not live to develop it, here was further evidence of a mind in advance of its time. Five years later a tandem-winged steam ornithopter, incorporating his research, would lift itself off the ground at the Crystal Palace Exhibition!

Sifting through the memorabilia was a sad endeavor for Elizabeth. Since the death of her parents there had been no one she had cherished more than her uncle, until Holmes came into her life at Brompton. Her sadness was heightened when, from a bureau drawer, she extracted a photograph, a theatre playbill, and a press cutting. They brought back memories too terrible for tears. The photograph had been taken for theatrical publicity purposes; it showed her parents, Simon and Sophie Lord, as they had appeared in a production of *Romeo and Juliet*. They were touring America in the play when tragedy struck, leaving Elizabeth an orphan.

Star-crossed lovers in every sense, this handsome couple had been publicly adored, a sentiment at odds with the turmoil of their private lives. The roles they played offstage parodied the public image of them as lifelong sweethearts; in fact, though deeply in love, they were incompatible. Had it not been for Elizabeth, whom they always took on tour, they probably would have parted. On the Sunday before they were due to open in Philadelphia, they went to the theatre for a last-minute run-through of the balcony scene.

Except for a spotlight onstage, the theatre was in darkness; all front-of-house doors were locked. While they rehearsed, an assistant stage manager entered by the stage door; it was his custom to bring food to the theatre cat at weekends. He lit a candle which, on leaving, he neglected to blow out. The cat must have knocked it over . . .

The press cutting told the grim story. Flames had so rapidly engulfed the theatre, in particular the stage-door area where it had started, that the couple perished in their effort to escape.

When Waxflatter arrived in Philadelphia ten days later after a dash across the Atlantic, he went to the theatrical lodging house where the Lords had stayed. He found a little girl of eleven fretting for her parents. Members of the company had kept the tragic news from her. The kindly uncle told her he had come to take her home. Only then did she learn the reason.

Elizabeth consigned these sad souvenirs to the locker. When her work was done, she began to worry about Holmes. No doubt she was concerned for my welfare too, but it was only natural that he should be in the forefront of her mind. Their love, I believe, owed something to the fact that each of them had known a less than happy childhood. Coming to terms with it was a background they shared. Each had developed an independent spirit, a quality each recognized in the other. The sufferings of Elizabeth's childhood were made clear to me by the items from the attic. I was to learn of the shadow that had clouded Holmes's, and the significance of his hallucinations in the church-yard, from a conversation we had while returning to Brompton from Oxfordshire.

We were within walking distance of the school and I was feeling the cold intensely. In the sub-zero condi-tions of that December, even the Thames had frozen in places, and there seemed no prospect of improvement. Holmes was immune to the cold, fuelled by that inner energy so exhausting to his friends. But I was feeling really miserable as we trudged on past the Serpen-tine.

"I should be at home in Carlisle," I heard myself muttering beneath my breath. "It's Christmastime and here I am walking through the night with a gang of fanatics on our trail. And I'm going to be expelled from school! Good Lord, Holmes! What have you got me into?"

He did not bother to reply. Now and then he stopped in his tracks, stared at the Rame Tep symbol on the letter Cragwitch had received, and muttered to himself: "Eh Tar! Rame Tep! Eh Tar!" The case in hand so absorbed him that he had no sympathy for me. This made me furious.

I flared up ill-humouredly. "Can't you think of anything else?" I don't think he even heard. "Investigating! Deducting! Rame Tep! Eh Tar! I'm sick of the whole bally business. And I am even more sick of you!"

At least I had got that out of my system. I felt less than proud as I reached deep into my pocket. There is nothing like a mint humbug on such occasions.

"I beg your pardon, Watson?" That showed that he had listened to my outburst.

"I am sick of you," I repeated with much petulance. "I am positively sick to death of you, Holmes."

"Now, now, Watson." His voice was very good-humoured. "You must watch your sugar intake."

"Rubbish," I snapped.

"I mean it, Watson." He said this in his pleasantest way. "You are bound to be a bit surly if you eat too many sweet things. 'Sweet tooth maketh a sour disposition.' That is an old wives' saying, but I believe it to be true. Haven't you heard it said?"

"I'm not interested in old wives' sayings." He was irritating me. "I don't think I have a sour disposition. I just need a good night's sleep."

"No more mint humbugs for you," he chided.

My patience was at an end. "There you go again, Holmes, always making smug pronouncements. Always criticizing me. You pounce on the tiniest flaw."

I had become so heated, debilitated from want of sleep, that I could hardly control myself. I felt I had good reason. Was it natural for Holmes, who was merely a year or two my senior, to be so obsessed with riddles and answers and so intent on solving this case? Could he not now leave Scotland Yard to unravel the mystery and bring the villains to book? It seemed to me unhealthy and dangerous for us to be so deeply involved. After all, we were schoolboys. We should have been thinking of Christmas, the season of goodwill, when families came together. It did not occur to me at the time that Christmas might have little meaning for him or that he might have no hearth to go to.

He turned to me. "I was trying to be dutiful, Watson," he said. "It is important to point out the error of a high sugar intake. It was the advice of a friend." His breath misted in the bitter air, his eyes showed concern.

I felt quite humbled. He was genuinely surprised that I had misunderstood him.

"Well, it is rather annoying to be treated so," I said. "I am not a child. I am nearly as old as you. What made you like this, Holmes? There has to be a reason. Most people aren't born with minds like yours. Nobody else I know has the ability to identify fifteen types of shoe leather or has made a study of body tattoos. Your knowledge of invisible inks and the footprints of squirrels is really rather unique. It's not normal, Holmes. You must admit it is unnatural."

"There are only fourteen types of shoe leather, Watson," he replied.

"See what I mean? You always have to be so damnably precise. Does it really matter? Must you be so sure of everything? We are not all born with minds like reference books, Holmes, crammed with curious detail. Nor are most people obsessed with analysis and deduction. What made you the perpetual sleuth?"

He looked at me sadly; I had not meant to wound. "Do you really want to know?" he asked.

"I do," I replied without rancour. "Yes, Holmes, I really do."

We resumed our walk and he began to unfold his story.

"I was eleven at the time, I remember. My parents were not old. They had married in their teens. But it was a marriage to which my mother's family had been opposed. They must have loved one another. Yet I could not recall a time when they had been happy. Something was very wrong, now. The marriage was in trouble. Even at my age I knew that."

"Children are very perceptive, Holmes," I said.

"They are sensitive to moods and atmospheres," he said. "Watson, have you ever kept a cat?"

I was so surprised by the question that I stood still and looked at him. While doing so I noticed that the cut Rathe's ring had made on his cheek had not entirely healed. It was like a scratch from a claw. "We have a cat at home," I said.

"So did we," he continued. "An old Siamese called Mehatabel. He was of great interest to me. I became a cat watcher. He was very wise. Mind you, he was watching me, too. They are like children, you know. He knew when I was unhappy just as I knew when my mother was. She tried to hide her feelings. It was no good. And I think she knew that I knew."

He brightened suddenly. "Watson, here is a riddle:

> 'Here I lie with my daughters
> A victim of impure spa waters.
> Had I stuck to Epsom salts
> We would not be in these vaults!' "

I began to think he was losing his mind.

"Which spa does that refer to?" he enquired.

"Really, Holmes," I said. "How should I know? I am not acquainted with English spas."

"The couplet refers to Cheltenham," he said. "During the Regency it was one of our most fashionable spas. But by mid-century the waters had become polluted, which was an omen because socially the place was changing too—not for the better, the old country families believed. The gentry resented the fact that the town was filling up with strangers. Anglo-Indian families were settling there after lives spent abroad."

"What was wrong with that?"

"The gentry looked down on them. They were not the kinds of persons they put on their invitation lists. They were forever boasting of their lifestyle in India where they had ruled the roost and servants abounded. They couldn't afford servants in England. The retired folk from India thought the gentry snobbishly unsociable. The gentry considered the newcomers beyond the pail. It was not a good mix."

"But, Holmes," I said. "What has the social history of Cheltenham got to do with your interests in detection? How did that come about?"

"It has everything to do with it, Watson, as you will see if you will be patient and listen. Mother came from an old country family, Father from an Anglo-Indian one. His father had been in the Indian army in Delhi; he had married a half-caste there. When my mother and father married, her people behaved very badly. It was as if they were ashamed of him. Although Mother was devoted, this affected him in many subtle ways. He hated the narrow outlook and social conventions of the place, its gossip; it was a world that seemed to spin around social status. We loved him, Mycroft and I, but he was never at ease with us. The contempt of my mother's family had actually managed to make him feel inferior. He never really succeeded in anything. I believe he would have become a brilliant lawyer if he had stuck to it. He was always on the side of outsiders, a champion of the underdog, but in Cheltenham society he was made to feel a rank outsider, himself. He became a bit of an idler; he drank a lot at times, and he started leaving home for days on end."

Holmes's voice trembled with the stress of these recollections. I kept my eyes on the road. He continued:

"Mother fretted terribly. I sensed how long the days were for her. When Father went away, the nights must have been even harder to endure. She was sleeping badly. Her beauty began to fade. Her only consolation was in her sons. I believe I was her favorite. I have always felt rather guilty about that. Mycroft is such an excellent fellow. She bought me presents. She often neglected him. She took me wherever she went and smothered me with love. Poor Mycroft. But you know, Watson, a son cannot compensate for the loss of a husband's love. I knew she was missing him.

"She kept busy. She was a great reader. She encouraged me to be. There were always books about. She played the piano with accomplishment, laments that echoed her unhappiness. But I owe my own love of music to her. Yet the strain was taking a toll. She was often ill. She seemed to be wasting away."

He was silent for a moment. These memories were hurting.

"The crisis came one night when my father returned from an unexplained journey. I don't think he even

182

troubled to make excuses or invent explanations. Mycroft was then at boarding school. I know that I began to cry in my room when I heard their raised voices. A bitter quarrel was proceeding, shattering irreparably any hope of tranquility. She was accusing him of seeing other women, of having affairs with them, and although he denied the charge, I knew they were breaking up."

"Poor Holmes," I said.

"No, Watson. Holmes had decided to do something about it."

"What could you do?" I asked. "What could a child do in such circumstances?"

"I decided to prove my mother wrong. I did not believe my father was being unfaithful. I knew he thought of himself as a failure. That was the reason he went away, I was sure of it. I had convinced myself that this was the explanation. Of course it was not something he could say to Mother; he was too proud. Besides, he had denied that he loved another woman. My aim was to prove he was telling the truth."

"How did you set about it?"

"I became a detective, Watson. I watched every movement he made. When he was at home I observed every detail, his manner, his appearance, everything he said. If he had returned from a mysterious journey, I was even more clinical in my observance of him. I was looking for clues to prove him innocent. I had set myself up as his judge. Was it Mother's hair on his lapel? Were his shoes worn down from walking? Did his skin show signs of exposure to the sun? Was the shirt he wore of a kind he had selected or had it been chosen for him? It was a matter of observation and deduction. And it became an obsession."

"I understand," I said.

"The logical next step was to follow him. I told Mother I was going on an outing with my friend, Tom Smith. That was the name I invented for a companion. She believed I was going to London to visit museums, art galleries, or the zoo with him. She approved of these expeditions. More than once she invited my fictitious friend to tea."

"With my pocket money I bought third-class tickets for trains in which I knew my father to be travelling. I became very adept at trailing him, expert in not being seen. I also became acquainted with the streets of central London. At the end of a day I knew his every movement. I was patiently observant. I even began to enjoy it; it had become a game, this stalking of a quarry through the city streets. Yet I was a hunter who did not want to reach his prey. I did not want there to be another woman."

"Was there?" I asked gently.

"One sweltering summer evening in Mayfair I was watching a certain mews off Curzon Street. I had seen my father enter a door that led up some stairs. He had used a key. For two hours I waited, dreading what I might see when the time came for him to leave. When he reappeared he was not alone. On his arm was a beautiful woman. They were smiling. She was radiant. They were undoubtedly in love. I can see her now. She bore an uncanny resemblance to my mother before the illness and the worry. I felt no sense of triumph, just an indescribable despair."

"Did you tell your mother?"

"I regret to say I did. To this day I don't know if I was right to do so. Remember, I was a confused, unhappy child. Before telling Mother, I confronted

Father. I accused him. He said I was mistaken. I could not possibly have seen him in Mayfair; he had been dining in Bayswater at the time. I said he was lying; I hated the sound of my words. I loved him dearly. Then, with infinite sadness, he confessed. He loved another woman."

"What did your mother do?"

"She left my father," Holmes said. "Mycroft and I went to live with her family. I have never felt really at home with them."

"So that is how you became a detective."

"Exactly, it all started then. I got into the habit. It has never left me. I began to read everything I could find relating to the subject—crime stories, memoirs, accounts of trials. You see, it is the fallibility of people which intrigues me. Because that is the key to human nature. We can all see what is on the surface. That is extremely simple. It is the underside of life which fascinates me."

"Since meeting you it has fascinated me," I said. "But with you it is an obsession."

"I admit that. I have bared my soul to you, it seems. I have told you how it started, this concern for the hidden motive, this search for unseen truths. You may at times have thought I was showing off. But it is my abiding interest. Perhaps it is also my curse."

"Not a curse, Holmes," I said. "Let us call it a magnificent obsession."

This remark pleased him. He brightened and was less tense. "Well, Watson, that is enough of the past. We must return to the case in hand. Who the devil is Eh Tar?"

We were silent for some time. Soon we were within sight of the school wall. It would be necessary to climb it if Holmes was to enter unseen. As we were preparing to do so, I saw him put a hand to his cheek. The scar had started to bleed. It reminded him of Rathe.

"My God!" he exclaimed, blanching with excitement. "How could I have been so stupid? It's Rathe, of course. He is Eh Tar. Watson, the game is afoot!"

Chapter Fourteen

AFTER WALKING UNCAS IN THE COURTYARD, TAKING care not to be seen, Elizabeth tried to relax on her uncle's favourite old sofa and waited for our return. She had drawn the curtains behind it and all was still in the early hours of the morning. But her labours in the attic, which had brought back so many memories, had fatigued her. If she nodded off, she told herself, Uncas would warn her of our approach.

She called to the faithful little terrier, but he would not settle. Something was worrying him. He trotted about the attic restlessly. He snarled by the front door, then ran to the curtained window. Some instinct seemed to be saying that all was not well.

Animals, she knew, possess senses which are no longer acute in humans due to our neglect of them. They seem able to perceive disturbing presences which we, to our peril, cannot. Was Uncas's sixth sense at work now?

"Come here," she called. "Come and join me." But the terrier continued to whine. He was making her nervous too, but she refused to believe in ghosts. No doubt the dog was simply anxious for Holmes to return.

She had to try to sleep. She was so desperately in need. She nodded off, only to be alerted by a rustling sound. Then came that dreadful jingling. Wide-awake at once, she noticed that Uncas's coat was bristling. Then both mistress and dog stiffened. From behind the curtain came a hand which rested on her shoulder. She was too frightened even to scream. When the wrist was revealed she saw that it wore a bracelet from which hung an amulet—a head of an Egyptian god. The curtains parted. There stood Mrs. Dribb.

At first she thought some absurd charade was in progress. She knew Mrs. Dribb and had some respect for her. Despite the sternness she had shown after their discovery the previous evening, she was still the school's kindly matron. When the boys got sick she ministered to them, she listened with sympathy to their problems, she bandaged their wounds. So for all her shock and incomprehension, Elizabeth waited for an explanation.

But she was to wait in vain. In no time at all Mrs. Dribb made her intentions unmistakably clear: they were violently aggressive. She seized Elizabeth in an armhold and tried to pin her down. The strength she used belied her gentle reputation and the girl was too astonished to resist.

Uncas, however, had harboured no such doubts or inhibitions. When the matron attacked, the dog was swift to defend his mistress. He grabbed the matron's skirt and ripped it; in brushing him off, Mrs. Dribb slipped and fell heavily to the floor. Uncas resumed the attack and the prone woman lunged at him like a wildcat. Uncas was decidedly more agile. Besides, he had found his enemy's weak spot. That thick bun of hair on the crown of the matron's head was immensely inviting. He bit hard into it. And to Elizabeth's surprise and to the delight of the dog, it came away in his teeth. Uncas ran off in triumphant possession of it. Mrs. Dribb had worn a wig.

But there was no real cause for satisfaction. Bereft of her wig the bald matron was even more frightening. Her head was shaven, except for a green strand which had been cut in the shape of a serpent. This epitome of compassion, this erstwhile Florence Nightingale—was a disciple of Rame Tep!

At last Elizabeth managed a scream. She bolted for the door, followed by Uncas. It opened as she reached it. She came face-to-face with Rathe. What a relief it was to see him! She appealed to him urgently. "Look sir," she said indicating the hairless matron. "Mrs. Dribb isn't what she seems. She belongs to a cruel sect. She is a murderess!"

His reaction was not what she had expected. That he should laugh at her was the very last straw. The awful truth began to dawn. He was a disciple, too. What he said confirmed this. "You have discovered our little secret. Now you must tell me where your friends are. Have they returned from their visit to the manor?"

Elizabeth was in despair. He had known all the time where Holmes had gone. Had he followed him there? Perhaps there had been foul play—or was he bluffing? Were Holmes and Watson in some trouble? The outrage of the deception amazed Elizabeth, but it also strengthened her resolve not to give anything away.

"You will never find them," she said defiantly.

Yet she could hardly believe it was happening. Rathe had been a hero to Holmes. Of all the masters at Brompton, Rathe was the one he had respected most, except perhaps for Waxflatter, but that was a regard based on sentiment as well as admiration for his pioneering research. To Holmes, the fencing master had symbolized fair play. He had admired Rathe's physical and mental coordination. Indeed, it was Holmes's philosophy too that a man should strive for perfection. It would not be an exaggeration to say that Rathe had been something of a superman to him.

What a shock it would be when he found out his real nature. Rathe was essentially evil. "You will never find Holmes," she repeated. "But he will find you."

Rathe's features remained passive. There was a suave smile on his face. He seemed quite indifferent to the fact that he and the matron had been unmasked. This girl's sensitivities were of no importance to him. But she did have importance; he had a very special use for her.

He began to move the hand on which he wore his unique ring, the one that had cut Holmes's cheek when it dazzled him during the fencing match. The sharp gleam of it now flashed across Elizabeth's eyes. He maintained a steady rhythm, moving it from side to side. Her eyes began to follow it back and forth, attracted by its lustre. He was hypnotizing her.

She made an effort to check herself, but the gleam was too powerful, too insistent. It was an anodyne that lulled her, relieving her of her fears, promoting a false sense of security. All she knew was a sensation of light and movement and an overwhelming need to sleep.

"You will never find him. He will find you." Was it her voice repeating these words? It seemed so far away. "Holmes, come quickly, I need you." But now there was no light anymore. She had surrendered. She had been hypnotized into a trance.

Mrs. Dribb was on her feet again. Uncas had made a fair old mess of her wig. He was rushing about, snarling and champing at their legs. The matron regained some of her dignity. "What shall we do with the girl?" she asked.

Rathe was surprised by the question. "Isn't that quite obvious? We have found our fifth princess."

His smile was now more sinister. She beamed with satisfaction.

They carried Elizabeth across the attic and down the stairs. "That wretched dog," said Rathe as they went, for Uncas was biting his ankles. "I wish you had impounded the little brute." He gave the dog a kick and it ran away howling. They took Elizabeth to a waiting coach.

Holmes and I had reached the wall when we saw the coach rush by. It was heading east toward the dockland. From the postilion, Rathe was whipping the horses into a frenzied gallop. Inside was Mrs. Dribb and the hypnotized Elizabeth. Holmes gasped. "My God," he said, "they are taking her to the temple! God knows what they will do to her there. They could even use her as a sacrifice. We must act quickly, Watson, if we are to save her."

"But how on earth can we?" I said despairingly. "They have such a good start on us."

"Never despair," Holmes replied, but it was dreadful to see his anxiety.

Suddenly the answer came.

"There is only one way to get to the temple in time," he said. "Watson, follow me. We are going to the roof."

"Holmes, you don't mean—"

He interrupted my question. "You have correctly guessed my intention. Yes, Watson, we are going to fly!"

Appalled though I was by the trouble Elizabeth was in, since I too was fond of her, Holmes's plan really scared me. As far as I was aware, Waxflatter's attempts to defy gravity had all ended in failure. Why should Holmes pin his hopes on the ornithopter?

He was brimming with confidence. He kept talking. I assumed it kept his mind from Elizabeth. "Gravity is an unrelenting adversary," he was saying as we made our way to the roof. "But this is our only chance. You see, Waxflatter was working on the wingspan problem right up to the day he died. Since then I've done some tinkering."

"Did he tell you what the problems were?" I felt I had a right to know.

"I think it concerned the length of the wings. He never made himself very clear. As I, he worked on intuition. You remember what the storekeeper said when the old boy lay dying at our feet? Little creatures with wings were attacking him. Subconsciously he was seeing little gremlins. They were what was wrong with his machine. It was the meaning of his hallucinations."

"Did he do anything about these gremlins?" I was keen to know.

"He had lengthened the wings."

By now we had reached the roof and Holmes began to examine the ornithopter.

"Do you see the modification he made to the port

wing?" I saw what looked like a bit of piping protruding from the tip of it. It made no sense to me.

"It will take the stress off the fuselage. Waxflatter knew his aerohydraulics."

It was all double-dutch to me. I had no wish to be a birdman. The ground is my natural habitat. Heights are anathema to me.

"Hopefully, all the bugs are out," he said as he strapped himself in. "If our work has been successful, we should be airborne soon. Prepare for take-off, my good friend."

"This is crazy, Holmes," I said.

At that moment Uncas appeared. He was wagging his tail at having found us. "Put him aboard, Watson," Holmes commanded, "and take the passenger seat, yourself."

To this day I cannot explain why I aquiesced. Holmes's enthusiasms were always difficult to resist, his confidence infectious. I was aboard a flying machine with a wholly inexperienced pilot and a little Jack Russell in my lap. I closed my eyes. There was a terrible shudder. I felt the airstream as we shot down the chute. Holmes was peddling madly, but the nose of the machine was pointing downward. He pedalled harder. It began to zigzag. It seemed to have a will of its own.

"For God's sake, Holmes, pedal even harder," I shouted. We were zooming in on West Brompton Station!

Then to our relief the ornithopter began to rise. We were airborne! In the freezing air, we were climbing. Up and up we went, deftly avoiding the Brompton Oratory and turning smoothly in the direction of the Houses of Parliament.

"It works," Holmes shouted. "It does actually fly!"

With relief we both began laughing, momentarily forgetting Elizabeth's mortal danger.

I tried not to distract him. "Turn right," I said quite sharply, for I feared we were not high enough to miss Big Ben. "As a matter of fact," I went on, "we should be going in the other direction. It would be best to travel up the Strand. Then we can look for the Tower of London." He looked displeased. "I am only trying to be helpful, Holmes," I said.

As a matter of fact, I was quite pleased with myself. I seemed to have related nicely to the role of navigator. I was actually enjoying the experience. Someday, I conjectured, oceans and continents would be crossed by this means. There is always excitement in being first. Suddenly I was thrust out of my complacency. "Holmes, for heaven's sake, fly higher!" We had almost crashed into Charing Cross railway bridge. "Your most direct route is to fly along the Thames," I advised. "Just follow the river, Holmes."

"Isn't it marvellous?" he shouted above the airstream. We could not hear the city's roar. Down there, London was silent, laid out for us like a toy.

"Just concentrate on the flying," I said.

I set my watch by the clock on St. Paul's and sucked a humbug. It was a quarter to five.

Despite an apparent calm, I would have liked to pray. Not being overly religious I did not know which God to appeal to. I might have settled for Icarus; but on second thoughts, not. He was flying's original casualty. He had been the first to crash.

Chapter Fifteen

BELOW US THE GREAT SNOW-COVERED CITY WAS awakening. It was still two hours from dawn, yet there were many upturned faces. We must have looked to them like some great predatory bird from prehistoric times. They looked up in wonder, unable to believe their eyes. I saw a clerical figure cross himself; lovers in a park ran for shelter, an errand boy toppled from his bicycle, and a little girl looked bravely from a window and waved.

It is marvellous what you can see from the air. This extraordinary journey, my debut as a flyer, was giving me a completely new perspective. I have wondered since then what our planet must look like from distant stars. Will our little world be visited centuries hence? Will there be encounters of an extraterrestial kind?

We were nearly there. "Can you land this contraption?" I shouted.

Our attention was diverted. On the ground below we spotted what looked like Rathe's carriage galloping through Aldgate at an alarming speed.

"What did you say, Watson?"

I was about to repeat my question when he interjected. "One moment, Watson, if you please. I was about to tell you that I have absolutely no idea how to land this thing."

My heart sank, but I remained vigilant. We were now at a lower altitude and the warehouse was directly below. We saw Rathe's coach arrive. He dismounted and Mrs. Dribb helped Elizabeth to alight. It was as if the poor girl were sleepwalking, so deeply was she hypnotized.

"Hold tight, Watson. We are about to land." I refused to look.

He was now back-pedalling. A rush of air from a different direction lifted the nose of the craft. Uncas pressed in closer. We were stalling. "We are going to hit the warehouse," I cried.

Holmes pedalled furiously and by some miracle got the machine under control. We were descending smoothly—down, down, down into the frozen Thames!

The impact broke the ice around us. The machine ploughed into the freezing water. We got out just in time and leapt from ice-flow to ice-flow, Uncas at our heels, until we reached the bank. Then we turned and saw the craft disappearing. Within seconds it had vanished. Nothing remained of Waxflatter's ornithopter. Not a single trace—which may well be the reason why history has no record of it.

We had no time for regret. "Come, Watson, hurry. We must get into the temple."

We went to where we had previously seen the conelike top of the pyramid. We had supposed it to be made of granite. Holmes thought differently now. "It may well be a theatrical mock-up. Be so good as to hand me that tool."

Nearby was an implement that coopers use to bind the staves of barrels. With this he chipped at the base of the cone. He was right; it was made of wood. It lifted from the main structure.

When we looked down, our worst fears were confirmed. Elizabeth had been led to the altar to be mummified.

A high priest flanked the assembly. Nearby were five coffins. Only one was empty and it was clear for whom that was intended. Before he put on the mask of Osiris we could see that the high priest was Rathe.

Never would I see Holmes more emotional. "They are going to murder her," he said. Then courage returned and he became the man of action. He lowered himself through the hole. "Watson, go to the basement. There is a way to the temple through there."

I followed his instructions and hid behind a pillar. Holmes was climbing down an iron chain which held the huge chandelier. So engrossed were they in their ritual that neither Rathe nor his disciples saw him. But the swaying chandelier cast a shadow and one disciple left to investigate. I realized it was Mrs. Dribb.

Holmes was trying to reach a lever which would lower the chandelier to the ground. But Mrs. Dribb was watching from the aperture above. She aimed a dart, but on seeing that it had missed, she took a flying leap and joined him on the chandelier. They fought tooth and nail for possession of the blowpipe.

When Rathe saw what was happening he urged the embalmers to work faster. Soon Elizabeth was being led to the coffin.

I made my way to the back of the altar. From behind

a tapestry I could see the hapless girl. I was poised for a dash to free her when all hell broke loose.

Mrs. Dribb, hit by a dart, fell screaming to the floor. The chandelier broke from the ceiling and it too crashed down. It scattered candles on the congregation and set tapestries aflame. Soon the temple was ablaze.

I seized an abandoned sword and rushed to help Elizabeth, but Rathe got there before me, grasped hold of her, and fled. Enmeshed in the iron chain, Holmes lay helpless on the floor.

I found a length of rope and looped one end around him. Trailing the other I pursued Rathe to his carriage where he was busy stowing in Elizabeth. He looked contemptuously at me and mounted the driver's seat. I fixed the rope to a rear axle and, to my relief, the tactic worked. For when Rathe started his horses, the rope detached the passenger seat, leaving him to gallop away with the front part of the coach. It also pulled Holmes to safety from the burning temple.

We lost no time in rescuing Elizabeth, but while she and Holmes embraced, Rathe reappeared on the scene. In one hand he held a gun, in the other a sword. Holmes had his back to him. Only Elizabeth could see what he intended. She thrust Holmes aside and the bullet hit her instead. Rathe ran towards the river.

We carried her to the wharfside and seated her as comfortably as the desolate place allowed. "You will be all right," Holmes told her, unaware that she was badly hurt. "Stay with her, Watson, I am going after that fiend." He picked up the sword I had carried.

She reached out a hand. "Holmes . . ."

He hesitated.

She beckoned him to leave. "I will wait," she said. But I sensed she was mortally wounded. . . .

Through all the years I knew him, Holmes would remain reticent on the subject of his final duel with Rathe. From what little I could see from the wharfside, and from the evidence of his wounds, it was a desperate affair.

In my concern for the plight of the dying girl, I could merely glimpse the combat, silhouetted in the first rays of dawn. But it lost none of its high drama as the two closely matched opponents fought first on the dockside and then on the frozen river.

When it began, the duel had a quality of athletic grace as all true swordsmanship should have between men of chivalry. For this is a sport as old as recorded history. Indeed, a relief carving in the temple of Madinet-Habu, built two thousand years before Christ, near Luxor in Upper Egypt, depicts a fencing match, and certainly all the ancient peoples from the Persians to the Romans practised swordsmanship in sport and war.

But such was Holmes's hatred for Rathe and Rathe's enmity towards him that the contest was a fight to the death.

It seemed to me, from my distance, that neither man could win, though they fought as if possessed. They lunged with reckless fury, locked swords and disengaged; their weapons resembled the antlers of stags in rut. Thrusts which would have felled less skillful men were given and received, and the clash of heavy metal echoed through the dawn air.

Then I saw one of them fall from the dockside onto the deck of a tethered boat that had been raised above the water. It slanted from the river wall. I did not know which man had fallen, but he was soon joined by the other. Then Rathe severed the tethering rope with a mighty blow and the boat slid from its mooring.

The impact cracked the ice. The boat disappeared below. Now the men were duelling on the ice floes, inflicting savage wounds. In a move I thought to be cowardly, Rathe shed his tweed cape and flung it towards Holmes in an attempt to blind him. But the younger man avoided it, grabbed the capes, and countered so savagely that the blow took Rathe by surprise. He appeared to drop his sword, lose his footing, and fall back on the breaking ice.

I waited tensely. Rathe did not reappear. The river had taken him. Then Holmes threw his own sword into the river. It was a gesture of contempt. He picked up the cape and came toward us.

His appearance displayed no triumph. Elizabeth was his only concern.

He knelt to her and took her in his arms. I turned aside gravely.

"There is no need for sadness," I heard her faint voice say. "You and I have been fortunate, Holmes. We have loved, a love that was pure. I will wait for you." She did not speak again. She was motionless. Elizabeth was dead.

I stood beside Holmes. He was weeping. I wanted to console him, but no words of mine seemed adequate. Helplessly, I gazed across the river.

A dark figure was emerging from the waters and scrambling up the bank. Holmes saw it too. "It must be Rathe," he said dejectedly, but there was nothing we could do. The figure disappeared into woods on the opposite shore. Holmes was too spent to follow. In any case, at that moment a posse of police arrived, Lestrade in command. He despatched fire-fighting vehicles to the burning temple. We knew every vestige had been destroyed.

Lestrade assessed the situation. Give him his due, when he realized the tragic circumstances, he attempted to console Holmes. But after a last look at Elizabeth, Holmes turned sadly away. The nightmare of Rame Tep was over but at far too great a cost. "Come, Watson," he said, linking arms. "We can leave this wretched place now." He would need every ounce of his courage to face the new day.

"You can leave it to us now, Holmes," we heard Lestrade saying. "We are rounding up those Rame Tep people who haven't perished in the temple. Thank you, Holmes." In this way he dismissed us. But by then we did not care.

Chapter Sixteen

As admirers of Holmes well know, it has invariably been my custom to conclude an account of a case by asking him how he arrived at certain conclusions during the course of it. This should be no exception to what would prove a general rule.

"When did you first suspect that Rathe was connected with Rame Tep?"

"The very first time we visited the temple," he replied. "He must have been there. How else would he know that I had not left London, following my expulsion?"

"And when did you know that Rathe and Eh Tar were one?"

"When my cut began to bleed. I was reminded of Rathe's ring, which bore the Rame Tep emblem."

"Were those your only clues?"

"No. I connected Rathe's presence at the school with that of Waxflatter. All members of the Cairo consortium were to get in touch with him. This put Rathe in touch with them, too."

"Why did the Egyptians wait so long before taking their revenge?"

"They had to wait one generation. The first eligible son, following the carnage at the tombs, was sent on a different mission. There was more urgent business. A little matter of an assassination in Tibet. They named the eligible son of the next generation Eh Tar and sent him to Europe for his education. Then he came to England to organize the recruitment of the cult and build a temple."

"Who was Mrs. Dribb?"

"She was Eh Tar's sister. Rathe obtained for her the post of matron at the school."

"Why did we not hear the jingling when she went about her school duties?"

"That puzzled me," he admitted, "until I realized that her uniform fitted so tightly, particularly around the wrists, that it prevented movement of the bracelet and, incidentally, hid it from view."

"Amazing, Holmes," I said.

"Elementary, my dear Watson."

"But you did overlook one further clue," I ventured.

"Please enlighten me," he said.

"Spell Rathe backwards, Holmes."

"Why, yes, it becomes Eh Tar!"

He was disconcerted but saved the day with impudence. "You have the makings of a detective," he said.

"Holmes," I said, "it is Christmas and I come bearing a gift."

He already wore Rathe's cape as a trophy and the old professor's deerstalker cap. Now I presented him with my pipe. Thus adorned, he looked most distinguished. "That is how I shall remember you," I said.

Then I recalled the riddle. "Holmes, the bear is white."

"Your reasoning?"

"Where else would you find a house affording only views to the south? At the North Pole, of course. So it is a polar bear."

"Well done, Watson." Even Uncas wagged his tail.

. . . Well, all that was long ago. Now even the years we spent at Baker Street are in the past. And Holmes is a figure of world renown.

It is some time since I have seen him. My wife has become more possessive with the passage of time. She likes me to be at home. That may well be to the benefit of a man of my years. But one fine autumn evening a month or so ago, I found my footsteps leading me in the direction of Baker Street. I was tempted to call but thought better of it. Perhaps Holmes too now lived with his dreams.

But I could not help but wonder if things had changed. Did he still keep his cigars in the coal scuttle, his tobacco in a Persian slipper? Were those great volumes of scrapbooks in their usual disarray? Were there still bullet marks on the wall? I could almost see him entering my bedroom with a candle in his hand, rousing me from slumber to join him on a new case. "Watson, the game is afoot!" he would exclaim.

"You are my one fixed point in a changing scene," he once told me. But what defence against change had he now? He had never married.

I returned to Kensington to my anxiously waiting

wife. But while crossing Hyde Park I imagined that I was being followed, at least by a host of memories.

"I saw no one," I would have told Holmes.

"That is what you may expect to see when I follow you," would have been his reply.

ACKNOWLEDGMENTS

ALTHOUGH THERE HAVE BEEN MANY SO-CALLED
Sherlock Holmes "pastiches," no one can make the
attempt without devoting study to Sir Arthur Conan
Doyle's stories. In doing so one gains a respect for
them and their creator which is quite profound. I
cannot adequately describe their ability to suspend
one's disbelief; it is a form of magic.

They are myths which linger in the consciousness.
They are for handing on to new generations who
inevitably become, in turn, devotees. If this narrative
is held to have integrity, it will encourage the process.
That thought was in the minds of the men who made
the film. Along with the actors, they all respected the
creator of Sherlock Holmes.

I drew on other sources. Although in my youth I
lived in Cairo, I was not then sufficiently mature to
appreciate its wonders or to learn much about its
incomparable history. These five books guided me
through its antiquity and across its desert sands:

Ameila B. Edwards's *A Thousand Miles Up the Nile;* Wilfred Thesiger's classic *Arabian Sands; A Search in Secret Egypt,* by Dr. Paul Bruton; *Napoleon to Nasser* by Raymond Flower; and *The Penguin Guide to Ancient Egypt.*

I also consulted *Flight Through the Ages* by C. H. Gibbs-Smith and *Grand Hotel—The Golden Age of Palace Hotels,* by various hands and published by J. M. Dent and Sons, Ltd.

My feeling throughout has been one of the deepest respect for the writings of Sir Arthur Conan Doyle, for the creator as much as for his creations. I share with the purists an admiration for Holmes's qualities. One that is sometimes overlooked is that he was a Victorian and Edwardian gentleman. "We live in a utilitarian age," he once told Watson. "Chivalry is a medieval conception." But, then, he was as much the great detective as he was the medieval knight. That is how I think of him.

Alan Arnold